"I didn't plan to arrive when you were—" her throat constricted and she waved a hand in the direction of the aisle where he'd walked with his oh-so-suitable fiancée **"—rehearsing for your wedding."**

"No?" The single syllable carried a weight of distrust.

"No!" She took a slow breath and sought calm. "Can we sit?" She looked around at the couple of hard wooden chairs.

"I prefer to stand. I don't have much time. I'm needed elsewhere."

It was probably true. Yet it sounded like a personal insult. As if she were some footnote in his personal history that he'd rather forget.

Aurélie drew a deep breath. Telling herself it didn't matter that this man was royal. That she wasn't daunted by his fancy clothes or the fact she looked washed-out and travel-weary in old jeans.

"I came all this way because something's happened."

She faltered to a stop, horrified at how emotional she felt sharing her news with an uncaring stranger. She swiped her tongue around her dry lips and forced herself to continue.

"I'm pregnant, Lucien. You're going to be a father."

Growing up near the beach, **Annie West** spent lots of time observing tall, burnished lifeguards—early research! Now she spends her days fantasizing about gorgeous men and their love lives. Annie has been a reader all her life. She also loves travel, long walks, good company and great food. You can contact her at annie@annie-west.com or via PO Box 1041, Warners Bay, NSW 2282, Australia.

Books by Annie West

Harlequin Presents

Demanding His Desert Queen
Contracted to Her Greek Enemy
Claiming His Out-of-Bounds Bride
The Sheikh's Marriage Proclamation

Secret Heirs of Billionaires

Sheikh's Royal Baby Revelation

Sovereigns and Scandals

Revelations of a Secret Princess
The King's Bride by Arrangement

Visit the Author Profile page
at Harlequin.com for more titles.

Annie West

PREGNANT WITH HIS MAJESTY'S HEIR

HARLEQUIN®
PRESENTS®

Recycling programs
for this product may
not exist in your area.

ISBN-13: 978-1-335-40358-2

Pregnant with His Majesty's Heir

Copyright © 2021 by Annie West

This edition published by arrangement with Harlequin Books S.A.

For questions and comments about the quality of this book,
please contact us at CustomerService@Harlequin.com.

Harlequin Enterprises ULC
22 Adelaide St. West, 40th Floor
Toronto, Ontario M5H 4E3, Canada
www.Harlequin.com

Printed in U.S.A.

PREGNANT WITH
HIS MAJESTY'S HEIR

Aurélie and Lucien's story is for all of you who, like me, love a Cinderella story.

Happy reading!

CHAPTER ONE

HE'D BARELY MOVED. The man whose face would make a sculptor weep and women stare.

More than stare. A couple of young, confident women had ventured across the restaurant, all shiny smiles and eager body language, only to return to their table disappointed.

The man with the wide shoulders, brooding expression and stunning amber eyes beneath night-dark hair wasn't in the mood for company.

He wasn't surly and he'd been perfectly polite to Aurélie, more polite than a lot of customers, but when he wasn't speaking with her, his face settled into stark lines. Even the way he was backed into that corner alcove for two, with his broad back against the ancient stone wall, seemed somehow defensive. As if ready to repel unwanted intrusion.

His face would be arresting at any time with those powerful, spare lines and generous mouth. But something about his sombre air and the pleat of a frown on his forehead caught Aurélie's attention. The way the frown intensified when his phone vibrated on the table. The way he refused to pick it up, spending the evening staring into space from under dark eyebrows or, occasionally, watching Aurélie as she wended through the tables.

It wasn't a busy night. So late in winter Annecy's tourist numbers had dropped. This town near the French Alps would attract them again as the weather warmed.

Aurélie told herself that was why her attention kept returning to Mr Tall, Dark and Handsome, because he was by far the most fascinating patron in the half empty restaurant.

She was honest enough to admit to a frisson of excitement as he'd followed her to his table. She'd been hyper-aware of his tall frame behind her and the intoxicating scent of the outdoors and warm male spice that tantalised when he passed her to take his seat.

Her awareness was grounded in intense attraction.

And something more. The conviction that something was wrong.

It was there in the whitened grip of his fingers around his drink. In the single-minded way he'd downed the first glass of wine as if he needed it badly. Yet now he seemed to have forgotten all about the drink in his hand. It was as if a dark cloud hovered over that corner, despite the dazzling effect of those stunning eyes and the couple of brief smiles he'd given her.

What would it be like if his smile reached his eyes?

Aurélie forced down a shiver of speculation as she cleared a table. The two Spanish guys had drunk their way through the meal and were ready to party. One still hadn't given up his determined flirtation. As she leaned forward, he lifted his hand as if reaching for her bottom. Instantly Aurélie tipped the plate she held. Another centimetre and he'd wear gooey cheese from leftover raclette. Meeting her stare, he raised his palm in apology.

From the corner of her eye she saw the man in the corner stiffen and put down his glass. Earlier, when the young Spaniard had first tried to touch her, the stranger had started to rise as if to intervene.

But she didn't need help. A few friendly but pointed words in Spanish reminded them that she wasn't on the menu. On the way to the kitchen she gave the man in the corner a discreet smile of acknowledgement. He responded with the tiniest tilt of his head.

Something caught hard in Aurélie's chest at the knowledge that he was watching out for her. She wasn't used to gallantry or protectiveness.

That had to be why her eyes kept seeking him out.

That and his aura of tightly restrained emotion. She felt it like a zap of energy whenever she approached his table. More so when those fiercely bright eyes locked on her, sending a shimmer of heat through her.

Or maybe she was projecting her own feelings onto him.

Her life was at a turning point. Opportunity lay ahead, but it had come at a cost. Stoically she told herself it was better to know than merely to sus-pect as she'd done for years. Yet it was hard hav-ing her suspicion proved true. That no matter how hard she tried she wasn't special enough to matter to those closest to her. She was on her own. Her family had finally stopped pretending otherwise.

Aurélie blinked and smiled at a customer look-ing to pay, ignoring the hollow ache behind her ribs. She refused to wallow in self-pity. She'd do what she'd always done, put her head down and work hard.

The difference was that now she had a real op-portunity for change. This time she'd grab it with both hands and make the most of it. It was time she stopped playing safe and took a chance.

Lucien watched the waitress beam at a customer, her smile lighting up her face. There was a radi-ance about the woman that kept drawing his gaze and dragging his thoughts from the well of dark-ness that encompassed him.

It wasn't just her dimple-cheeked grin as she swapped comments with customers in at least four different languages. Or the vibrant red hair, pulled back in a bouncing ponytail that gleamed like jew-els and firelight.

His eyes followed her quick, supple movements, a mix of grace and strength as she manoeuvred through the tables carrying laden plates. Then there was her easy humour. Even when that drunken lout tried to grope her, she'd used humour underscored by steel to put the guy in his place yet leave him smiling.

And sometimes, as if to remind Lucien that he wasn't completely cut off from the rest of the world, her eyes would catch on his. The effect was startling. Each time warmth began to trickle painfully through his frozen being.

Since the news had reached him this morning it felt as if a wall of ice separated him from the rest of the world. Lucien knew it was shock and when it wore off everything would be far too real.

Strangely, when she met his eyes, *that* connection felt real. She looked at him and he imagined he saw acceptance and understanding. A warmth that, despite his need to be alone with his grief, beckoned invitingly.

What he didn't see was the voracious eagerness those other women had shown when they'd come to his table uninvited. As if he'd make their raucous girls' night out complete.

Lucien couldn't imagine ever wanting to party again.

Not when his world was a yawning maw of hurt.

He frowned into his glass, swirling the liquid then downing it in one, heat spilling down his throat. Yet still he was chilled to the marrow. He'd thought alcohol might dampen the biting ache but it had no effect.

He kept imagining Justin, his car smashed by

the impact. And when he couldn't stand that, his brain conjured images of the trip they'd made here years ago. Justin had been ecstatic with his incognito escape. Lucien's memories of that time were filled with the sound of his cousin's laughter. At the simple joys of camping. At paragliding or sailing on the lake or drinking beer by a barbecue like two ordinary guys.

That was why Lucien had found himself turning off the *autoroute* and heading for this town in eastern France that was only marginally on the way to Vallort. They'd wanted him to fly straight there but he'd insisted on driving himself. Tomorrow would be time enough to face his grim responsibilities.

Tonight he needed to be alone with his memories.

First Uncle Joseph, the only father he'd ever known, had succumbed to what had at first seemed a mild illness. Then, less than twenty-four hours later, Justin, as close as any brother. Had his reflexes been impaired by grief over his father?

They were the last of Lucien's family.

He dragged in a breath laden with lacerating ice shards, despite the heat of the room. With it came skewering pain, lancing his chest, so sharp his lungs froze and the edges of his vision blackened.

Lucien lurched to his feet.

He needed to get out of here.

It was snowing when Aurélie left the restaurant. Soft plump flakes drifted across her cheeks and settled on her dark sleeves, making her smile. All around was silence, as if everyone else was tucked up snug and warm and she was the only one to witness the light fall.

Hugging her old coat closer, she stepped across the cobblestones towards the shallow river flowing through the heart of the old town. The Palais de l'Île was illuminated, its ancient stonework picturesque on its island in the centre of the river.

Would she miss this place when she left? Would she—

Movement at the corner of her vision made her turn. A tall form melded with an old wall but wasn't part of it.

In her pocket Aurélie's hand closed around her keys, threading them between clenched fingers. She'd always felt safe here even after a late finish, but it paid to be cautious.

She was turning away, deciding to take the long way to her tiny flat, when something about that shadowy figure made her pause.

He, for it was definitely he, looked familiar.

For three heartbeats she stood there, not sure why she hesitated, till her eyes adjusted to the gloom and she recognised him.

'*Monsieur?* Are you all right?'

It was him, the solitary customer who'd awakened her curiosity.

Aurélie realised he was coatless, wearing only jeans and a pullover. From the way the finely knitted fabric clung to him she'd wondered earlier if it might be cashmere. Certainly it was expensive. But it wasn't warm enough for standing out in the snow. How long had he been here? He'd left almost an hour ago. Snow had settled on his shoulders and dark hair.

She frowned. He could certainly afford a coat given the generous tip he'd left.

Aurélie took a step closer and saw a ripple pass through him. Like someone waking from sleep. Or someone on the verge of hypothermia?

'It's you.' His deep voice had a roughened quality she didn't recall from earlier. There was no threat in it. Instead it sounded rusty, as if his vocal cords had seized up.

'What are you doing here?' she probed.

Waiting for you.

She could imagine the young Spaniard saying that, grinning lasciviously.

'Just…thinking.' She heard him swallow. 'I needed some fresh air to…' His words petered out.

'To think.' She nodded briskly, telling herself she wasn't disappointed that he wasn't waiting for her.

Occasionally in the past a customer had, misinterpreting her professional friendliness for something else. Why was it that tonight she almost wished this man had?

Because tonight her professional smiles hid an awful emptiness. Because she felt alone, rebuffed, even betrayed by her family.

Because this man made her feel something powerful and different. As if they knew each other, despite being strangers.

Aurélie slammed a lid on such frivolous thoughts.
Frivolity had no place in her life.

'You can't think here. You'll freeze,' she said
briskly, taking another step closer.

His eyes were fixed on her but something about
his expression told her his thoughts were elsewhere.

'Where's your coat?'

He shrugged. 'In the car, I suppose.'

'Which is where?'

He nodded towards the lake in the distance. 'In
the underground car park.'

'Okay then, where are you staying tonight?'

'Staying?' Then, as if surfacing from deep water,
he shook his head and drew a deep breath. 'I'm not
sure. I was going to drive on after dinner but I had
no real plans.'

'You've been drinking. You can't drive any further tonight in case you cause an accident.'

His reaction shocked her. A great shudder ran
through him and he put out a hand to the wall beside him as if needing its support. He said something under his breath that Aurélie couldn't catch
but she didn't miss the note of searing anguish.

She'd been right. Something was wrong.

Closing the gap between them she briefly
touched his hand. Ice-cold. This close she saw the
way he shook.

'Are you sick?'

'No. Just cold.' He sounded surprised and she wondered if he even realised how long he'd stood out here.

'Have you taken drugs?'

'Of course not!' He straightened away from the wall, suddenly taller and more alert. 'I don't do drugs.' His voice was more normal too, as if he'd surfaced from whatever place his thoughts had led him.

Aurélie weighed her options, knowing her friends would tell her not to do what she was going to. That *she'd* advise any friend in similar circumstances to walk away. Yet she couldn't. Not tonight. Not with him.

It was inexplicable but she knew this was right.

'Come with me.' She turned on her heel.

'Where?'

'To my place.'

CHAPTER TWO

'You can have a hot drink and warm up and we'll
find you a safe place to stay.'

Lucien forced his stiff legs to work and followed
her quick steps down the narrow pedestrian street.

He wasn't used to taking orders. Usually he was
the one giving them. Tonight though, his heart was
full of grief. His mind was buffeted by the complete derailment of his life. By the problems awaiting him in Vallort. It was simpler to let this woman
issue her instructions.

Yes, a hot drink. He hadn't realised how cold he
was. He couldn't feel his feet and his cheeks and
ears felt frozen.

Yes, a place to stay. Dimly he realised he needed
that. Somewhere quiet where he could be anonymous. It would be his last quiet, anonymous night.
Suddenly that seemed incredibly precious.

From this point on there'd be no anonymity, at
least in his home country. Certainly no chances to
head off with friends after work for a party.

As for working late in his office… Lucien drew
a sharp breath. No doubt he'd spend many nights
working late but it wouldn't be at his architect's
desk and it wouldn't be on any of the projects he'd
planned.

All that would be denied him.

He grimaced, catching the direction of his thoughts.

How could he feel self-pity when Justin could feel nothing at all? When, in a couple of days, Justin and his father would be laid side by side in the family vault.

'Are you sure you don't need a doctor?' She'd stopped before a battered wooden door, the meagre light from a wall sconce making her hair glow.

'Quite sure.' Lucien made an attempt to escape his circling thoughts and focus. He frowned down at her. 'You don't know me. Do you think it safe to invite strangers home?' Her eyebrows arched as she stared up at him. 'Sorry. I don't mean to sound like your father.'

He didn't like the idea of someone taking advantage of her. Through the welter of old memories a new one surfaced, of that young tourist trying to grope her. Lucien's jaw tightened.

Her laugh was short and bitter. 'You don't sound at all like my father.'

Instinct nudged Lucien, telling him there was more to her words than was obvious, but already she was opening the door.

'Don't worry, I'm not inviting you here to have my wicked way with you.' Her words were sharp but her eyes slid from his. It struck him that she'd misinterpreted his concern as a jibe at her morals. 'I just don't want to come out tomorrow to find you frozen in a doorway. So, if you're coming, hurry up.'

No mistaking the snap in her words. Lucien silently cursed his clumsy tongue. The last thing he'd intended was to insult her. He liked her. And right now she felt like his only anchor to a sane and better world.

A couple of minutes later he stood in a tiny living space with the smallest excuse for a kitchen he'd ever seen tucked at one end.

She threw out an arm to one of two doorways and he felt a pang of disappointment that she didn't meet his eyes. He wanted her cautious with other men but not, he discovered, with him. 'That's the bathroom. There's a clean towel on the shelf. Help yourself to a shower to warm up while I make us hot drinks.'

'Thank you. You're very kind. I appreciate it.'

Lucien paused, willing her to turn. Finally she did and he saw wariness and a bruised look in her brown eyes. Had he hurt her? Tonight he felt clumsy, lost between the present and the past, having trouble expressing himself. It took a monumental effort to conjure a smile of thanks. His taut facial muscles protested, but he saw her expression ease a little.

She nodded towards the bathroom. 'And pass out your pullover. I'll put it near the radiator to dry.'

It was only then Lucien realised he was wet as well

as cold. In the warmth of this tiny space his clothes clung uncomfortably, the wool itching his skin.

'I'll give it to you now.' He hauled the wet wool up and over his head and held it out to her. 'Thanks.'

Then he took the couple of strides to the bathroom, telling himself he'd feel more himself when dry and warm.

Aurélie blinked as the bathroom door closed. Minutes later she heard the shower start up and realised he'd have to bend to fit under the spray. The flat was tiny and he dwarfed it. He was well over six feet tall.

And beautifully built.

Her thoughts strayed to his lean yet powerful-looking body. The play of muscles as he shrugged off his pullover then strolled away, loose-limbed and straight-shouldered. Aurélie's gaze had dropped to his perfectly rounded backside in black jeans and her mouth had dried.

No, it had dried when he smiled. Those amber eyes had warmed, crinkling at the corners, and she'd felt it like a punch to the middle.

As if no man had ever smiled at her before.

Never a man like that.

She wasn't sure what made him different.

Her mouth tugged into a rueful curve. Nothing apart from stunning looks, an aura of magnetism and a smile that transformed his face despite the lines of strain. And that air of brooding distraction that teased her curiosity.

Whatever it was, it made Aurélie realise with a sudden jab how isolated she was, despite her busy schedule and her plans for the future.

Even surrounded by family she'd felt unloved.

Now they'd gone and she realised she was actually *lonely*.

She had friends but they weren't very close since Aurélie had always been too busy juggling the demands of work and her family to enjoy a very active social life.

Was that why she'd taken pity on a stranger and risked bringing him here? So that, for the time it took him to finish a hot drink and warm up, she wouldn't be alone?

Aurélie stiffened. She wasn't so needy.

She looked down at the damp black wool, heavy in her hands. Her fingers twitched, registering residual body heat and that slight yet heady fragrance of masculine skin.

Nostrils flaring, she stalked across to the radiator and hung it over a nearby rail.

The drinks were ready when he emerged.

'That was terrific. Thank you, Ms…?'

'Aurélie.' She stirred his drink rather than stare at that honed body. 'I'm sorry I don't have a shirt to fit you, but your pullover should be dry soon.' As for his damp trousers, there was no way she was offering to dry those too. He needed to be at least semi-clothed.

'Thank you, Aurélie.' His deep voice turned her name into a lilting caress and a tiny shiver raced through her. 'I'm Lucien.'

She nodded and passed him a steaming mug, feeling crowded since he took up all the space, or at least all the oxygen in the room.

'Hot chocolate?' He sniffed the drink.

'I never have coffee at night. It takes me ages to unwind after a shift. Please—' she gestured to the small, lumpy sofa '—take a seat.' Because it was easier to think with some distance between them. She'd stay here, leaning against the benchtop.

'You play chess?' He gestured to the board on the crate that served as a coffee table. 'How about a game while I wait for my pullover to dry?'

Aurélie's gaze flickered from his sculpted profile to his bare chest with its fascinating dusting of dark hair. Chess would give her something to concentrate on rather than gawking at his body. Finally she nodded.

It didn't work as well as she'd hoped. Sitting close to him was distracting and Lucien beat her easily. But Aurélie found it surprisingly comfortable, sharing the night quiet with him. Her residual discomfort at rashly inviting a stranger here died as they spoke desultorily about chess and then about games they'd played as kids.

She learned he loved to ski and that he'd grown

up in the mountains, though, judging by his faint accent, not in France. Aurélie chose not to query him more closely. What was the point? He'd be gone soon. Tomorrow he'd be just a memory. Besides, he seemed so self-contained that any direct questions would feel like an intrusion on his privacy.

He heard about her love of music, that she'd wanted to play the piano but sang instead. Aurélie made that sound like a choice, not mentioning there'd been no money for music lessons.

When he suggested a second game she agreed, surprised when she won to discover how long they'd been playing. She felt relaxed with Lucien. Except for that tiny current of awareness running deep into the core of her body. He might be good company but he was still the most attractive man she'd ever met.

'Congratulations,' he murmured. 'There are flashes of real brilliance in your game.'

'Why, thank you.' Her smile died as she saw his hands clasped, white-knuckled between his knees. His mouth was a crooked line. 'Lucien, what's wrong?'

The man was in pain, no doubt about it.

'Nothing. You just reminded me of someone.' His jaw clenched so hard it was a wonder the bone didn't splinter.

'Another chess player?'

He nodded and she watched him swallow, his

Adam's apple jerking against the strong line of his throat.

It was none of her business. Whatever bothered him wasn't something she could solve. Yet Aurélie read stark misery on that proud face and felt its echo within her.

'Do you want to talk about it?'

He raised his head then, his eyes so bright they seemed to catch all the light in the room and drive it deep inside her where a confusion of emotions— pity, regret and the desire to comfort him—melded.

'Thanks.' His voice was a raw whisper. 'But it's too late. He's dead.'

'I'm sorry.' Aurélie knew about grief. Even after all these years, she remembered the loss of her mother, the pain so keen it defied belief. And then the long, lonely days that followed.

Aurélie couldn't bear to watch the way anguish etched his features. She leaned towards him then made herself stop.

'Someone close to you.' It was a statement, not a question, but he answered anyway.

'My cousin, but we were brought up like brothers.'

Aurélie's heart rolled over in her chest. How would she feel if one of her little brothers died? They'd grown up taking her for granted, as her father and stepmother did, relying on her rather than loving her. But still she cared for them. She'd be devastated to lose them.

'Sorry,' he murmured. 'You don't need this.'

'It's fine. Grief takes a long time. How long has it been?'

His mouth dragged up at one side in a grimace. His eyes met hers and again that blast of connection hit her like a drill bored right into her soul.

'I found out this morning.'

'Oh, Lucien!' Her heart wrung for him. He must feel raw inside.

Aurélie rose and took a seat beside him on the sofa. Tentatively she touched the back of his hand with her fingertips. She didn't want to intrude but there were times when human contact was important. This seemed one.

His skin was hot and his fist was clenched so hard it shook. She tried to ignore the sizzle of energy that shot through her from the point of contact, instead breathing deep and concentrating on him.

'I wish I could say something that would make a difference.'

He shook his head, a stray lock of espresso-dark hair falling across his brow. It made his sculpted features look almost boyish as he turned to look at her.

'You've already done so much. You brought me back. For a while there I felt completely lost.'

Beneath her fingertips his hand turned, palm up, and he laced his fingers with hers. Another ripple of sensation, stronger this time, shimmied up her arm. It spread warmth through her chest and lower, right down into the depths of her being.

What was this? She'd never felt anything like it.

'You feel it too.' His eyes held hers.

Aurélie felt trapped, caught by his bright gaze and disorientated by something within her that urged her to hold tight and not let go.

'Sorry?'

'This.' His hand squeezed hers and her breathing turned fluttery.

Aurélie stared back, overwhelmed by the need to stay connected. By a response to this man—this *stranger*—that was beyond anything she'd experienced.

'I don't understand you.' An instinct for self-preservation prompted the words.

For a second longer she felt it, the thrill of contact, his flesh against hers, his stunning eyes holding hers, then he moved. Her hand fell to the red upholstery and the blaze inside died a little as he turned away. Not only turned but surged to his feet.

'You're right. I shouldn't have… That was a mistake.' He raised his arm and forked his hand through his hair, pushing it back off his brow. Aurélie watched the mesmerising shift and play of his oblique muscles and others she couldn't name as he moved.

Moved away.

Her heart hammered to a stop so abruptly she felt sick, then it started up again, fast and erratic.

'What are you doing?' Aurélie was on her feet.

He didn't look at her. He wore that closed expression she'd seen in the restaurant and out on the street.

'Thanks for your hospitality, Aurélie. I appreciate it. Now it's time I left.'

'You can't go.' Her voice rose. 'It's not safe to drive and you haven't got a place to stay.' Why hadn't she made that a priority?

He shrugged and reached for his pullover. 'I'll sleep in the car. I have to leave now.'

Aurélie stood in front of him, forcing him to look at her. When he did, the impact of that glittering stare almost rocked her back on her feet. Yet it was nothing to the urgent emotions within.

'Why?'

He paused, hands fisting in the dark wool, his bare chest rising sharply on a ragged breath.

'Because I want you, Aurélie.'

He dragged in another breath that rasped loud in the silence while his words demolished something inside her.

'I've wanted you from the first moment you smiled and led me to my table. I watched you walk in front of me—your scent, the sway of your hips, the perfect curves of your backside...even the damned swing of your ponytail beckoned me.' His voice ground low, hitting a husky note that dragged through her like fingers raking velvet.

Lucien swallowed and she watched the movement, read urgency and mouth-drying hunger in the jerky action. It mirrored her own response to his words, his nearness. Her throat was parched, her heartbeat jagged and she felt strung out with anticipation.

Hadn't she spent the evening fascinated? *Wanting?* Trying to pretend that she didn't? Telling herself it was mere charity that led her to invite him here when from the first she'd been driven by another compulsion entirely?

'I thought I could control it. Be civilised and grateful and walk away. I *will* be all those things,' he added through clenched teeth, 'but I have to go *now*.'

Her hand closed on his bare arm and he went rigid, his breath like the hiss of water on molten metal. Surprisingly soft hair tickled her palm. She felt corded muscle and heat and again that singing, soaring sense of rightness.

'I feel it too.'

'What?' Finally he swung his head to look at her.

'I feel it. The connection. The…need.' Aurélie swallowed against the emotions constricting her throat. 'I don't understand it. I don't usually…'

She shook her head, bewildered by the strength of her feelings. Then, blessed relief, his other hand cupped her face, his touch fortifying and reassuring.

'I don't usually either.'

His expression was dead serious, despite the sexual tension twanging between them.

Aurélie lifted her chin. 'I hadn't realised how

alone I felt until tonight. When you came…' She paused, trying to find the words.

'When I came, what, Aurélie?'

She could listen to him saying her name for ever, in that smoke and suede voice that undid her every time.

'I can't explain.'

His thumb brushed her cheek, slowing to swipe her bottom lip. She shivered. It felt as if a fine wire tightened between her mouth and her breasts.

'Like there's a link between us?' he murmured.

'As if I recognised you, knew you, though you're a complete stranger.' It was a relief to admit it, however crazy it sounded. Her hand tightened on his arm. She revelled in the connection, as if claiming him.

'I feel the same.' He shook his head, his expression grave. 'I don't want to leave, Aurélie. I want to be with you. Spend the night making love to you.'

Relief was a sigh of breath as her lungs emptied then refilled.

'Yes.' A smile trembled on her lips. 'I want that too.'

Lightning flashed in his eyes and surely a jagged bolt struck her too. She felt the heat solder her feet to the floor.

'Aurélie.' He shook his head as if he couldn't quite believe it. 'You know I'm passing through. I won't be back—'

'Shh.' Her finger on his lips stopped his words.

'I know this is only for tonight.' She hesitated a second then added, 'I'm leaving here too. I don't think I'll return.'

It was the first time she'd said it out loud. It felt like crossing into unknown territory.

Whereas, remarkably, planning to have sex with a man she'd met just hours ago felt perfectly normal.

She needed this, needed Lucien with a force she couldn't comprehend yet couldn't doubt. Whatever the reason, this felt real and right.

For once she'd do something for herself, not because it was demanded by others. Just as, later, she'd move from the only town she'd known and begin the new life she'd dreamed about.

For one slow, delicious moment their gazes held and time stood still. Then Lucien bent his head and his mouth brushed hers, soft as a drifting snowflake, teasing her lips. Aurélie looped her arms around his neck and rose on tiptoe, responding, inviting, urging.

A second later her body was plastered against his, pulled close by strong arms lashing her to him. Lucien delved into her mouth and she welcomed him, stroking tongue against tongue, feeling a churning hollow ache low in her body as their kiss moved from tantalising to erotically charged in seconds.

His naked torso, the solidity of those hard thighs against her own, the absolute certainty of their kiss, as if they weren't strangers but lovers who'd been apart too long and came together instinctively—all made her long for more.

Aurélie had no recollection of moving to the bedroom. But stripping Lucien, *that* was clear in her mind. The sound of his zip louder than her drumming heartbeat. The drag of fabric down his hips to pool at his bare feet. The phenomenal heat of his lower body. That glimpse in the half-dark of his erection that made every feminine part of her soften in readiness.

His hands on her clothes were deft yet gentle. Her ears echoed with whispered words of praise as he eased off her shirt, kissing the bare flesh of her shoulder with a desperation she felt with every snatched breath.

Briefly she considered suggesting they take this slow, wondering if her limited experience might be a handicap. But the idea dissolved as his naked body touched hers. She didn't care about lack of technique when he lowered himself beside her, flesh against searing flesh.

Maybe it was Lucien who made this seem inevitable and perfect. Maybe it was a feminine instinct she'd barely been aware of previously. But there was no fumbling, no uncertainty.

Instead of covering her body with his, Lucien explored her with hands and mouth, learning what she liked. Which was everything, including the slide of his strong body down hers, making her pulse thrum and her breath catch. He worshipped her breasts with his mouth and watching him loosened something inside her, making her shudder with the need for release.

But she wasn't submissive. She was curious about his body, pleased when he let her push him onto his back so she could explore.

He was perfectly formed, taut, silky skin over muscle and bone, and she wanted to feast on him. Lucien gasped when she bit his earlobe and trailed her fingers across his hipbone. She moved lower, discovering the taste and texture of him. When she licked his nipple he muttered something gruff and unintelligible into her hair as his whole body trembled.

Aurélie took him in her hand, fascinated by the combination of velvet softness over iron-hard arousal. Trailing touches gave way to deliberate caresses, a tighter grip that made him sigh and his hand close over hers, guiding her. She loved giving him pleasure, watching his big form grow rigid. She was bending to take him in her mouth when he hauled her up his body, his hand between her legs turning her protest into a sigh of delight.

They didn't speak beyond fractured gasps or groans of pleasure and encouragement. Through it all ran a sense of rightness, that their coming together was as natural as spring following long, cold winter.

Aurélie blossomed beneath his touch and his tenderness. When, finally, Lucien sheathed himself

and settled between her thighs, his gaze holding
hers as their bodies merged, it was so easy it felt
like coming home.

Home to a wonderful place where every yearning was satisfied.

For long moments neither moved.

Then, abruptly, it was too much, the need for
completion too overwhelming.

Lucien moved and she rose to meet him, soles
planted on the mattress as she lifted into his caress.
Murmuring words of encouragement, he slid his
hand beneath her, bringing them into even closer
alignment. Control shattered. Their movements
quickened, his thrusts taking him deeper than she'd
thought possible as she clung to his wide shoulders.

Her brain scrambled, bombarded by so many sensations. The one constant was that amber gaze, holding her safe, as his body took her higher and higher
till their climax engulfed them simultaneously.

Passion escalated from glorious to sublime. The
world fell away and they became the whole uni-
verse, hearts beating in unison, mouths fused, bodies clinging as rapture stormed in, shattering them
and then reforming them again.

Her body, her mind, and even her soul, basked
in glory. And through it all she held Lucien close,
needing him but wanting to protect him too.

Lucien's heart raced, his whole body wrung out
from ecstasy, yet despite the exhaustion he felt

triumph and gratitude to the woman already fast asleep in his arms.

He should sleep too. They'd spent the whole night making love, tenderly then urgently, then with laughter and finally now, as grey dawn lightened the sky, with a silent, hungry passion that scoured him to the bone.

Because their night together could only be that, a solitary night.

It seemed preposterous when, with Aurélie, the woman whose surname he didn't know and never would, he'd discovered more than solace from grief. He'd found, somehow, the part of himself that had gone missing when he'd heard of Justin's death. He wasn't healed. His grief was too big for that, but Aurélie had given something of herself, or perhaps they'd created something miraculous together, that filled the gaping hole in his heart. At least enough for him to face what must be faced.

He smiled against her hair, inhaling her delicate floral scent, enjoying the way her unbound curls tickled his skin.

Or maybe his imagination was running riot because he'd just had the best sex of his life.

His smile flattened. No. It was more than that. It had been more than that from the moment he'd seen her. Sexual attraction was easy to identify. What he couldn't name was the other thing between them. It drew them like old friends reuniting or lovers together again after a long absence.

He huffed out a breath, half hoping Aurélie would wake. But she was out for the count. While he'd spent the evening brooding over his troubles, she'd been on her feet for hours, working.

Lucien recalled the touch of her hands on his body. They weren't soft hands, though they spun magic easily, whether tender or demanding. This was a woman who worked hard, not some pampered socialite.

His own hand slid down the amazing curves of her body, from her ribs to the tight sweep in to her waist then up her hip, lingering there as she shifted in her sleep and murmured something he couldn't catch.

It struck him that he'd give a lot to be able to do this again. Every night in fact. Imagine coming home to Aurélie. To those big brown eyes that seemed to understand so much. To her pragmatic, understated sympathy. To her warmth and generosity, her passion and...

Lucien slammed an iron door on his thoughts.

It couldn't be.

Even thinking about it could only bring regret and pain.

Softly he pressed one last kiss to the side of her neck, heard her sigh and felt her tiny wriggle against him, as if even in sleep she needed to be close.

He knew the feeling.

Slowly, determined not to wake her, he withdrew his arm from under her and slid out of the bed.

It took enormous willpower to dress and turn away. He paused in the minuscule living room, switching off the light they'd left burning all night.

As he did, his gaze went to the chess board. A pawn had dropped to the floor, probably when they'd kissed. It was hard and cold in his hand and for a moment Lucien felt again the desperation that had risen inside him yesterday, along with the grief of loss. He'd felt like a pawn, being shuffled around some cosmic chess board without the right to choose his own direction. His future was being mapped out for him by forces beyond his control.

This morning, as he placed the small piece on the board, his gaze swept to another piece, taller and distinctive.

He breathed out slowly, feeling his chest swell and fall. Now he felt the calm of acceptance. There was no use fighting fate. He had a duty to perform and he wouldn't shirk. Both his cousin and his uncle would have expected it of him. More, he knew in his heart that he'd never live with himself if he didn't do this, even if it felt like nothing but sacrifice.

He allowed himself one last look over his shoulder, heart squeezing at the picture of pale limbs and tumbled bright hair. Aurélie would only be a memory in his new life.

Lucien opened the door and quietly left.

CHAPTER THREE

A COUPLE OF months later Aurélie looked at the shabby backpack at her feet and wished she'd done the sensible thing and checked into a hostel as planned.

She'd had it worked out. Find somewhere cheap to stay. Have a hot shower after the long bus trip and change into the set of good clothes she'd bought.

But there were roadworks in the capital and the bus had taken a detour through the picturesque old town with its quaint buildings and arched lanes. When it stopped right before the Vallort royal palace it had seemed like providence and Aurélie had taken that as a positive sign.

Besides, today was one of the days part of the royal palace was open to the public. It was already late, due to delays on the journey. If she found a hostel and returned here she might be too late to get in.

So here she was, sitting on a gilt chair in the corner of a grand reception room, being stared at by a granite-faced guard. He and another staff member had told her multiple times that there was no point waiting. But wait she did, feeling totally out of place and more than a little daunted.

She'd tried before, via phone and email, but had been fobbed off. Speaking to a VIP who didn't want to talk to you or who hadn't told their staff to allow contact from you was impossible.

Aurélie leaned back in the uncomfortable chair and pretended interest in the frescoed ceiling which, according to the guidebook, was a masterpiece of baroque art.

Above her on the painted surface stood a figure draped in ermine, some grand King of Vallort, surrounded by courtiers and family. She scrutinised his face but, in his wig and regalia and wearing that expression of serene arrogance, he bore little resemblance to the man she'd come to see. Around him fat cherubs strung garlands and elegant women who wore nothing but fabric improbably draped around their hips looked on approvingly. Maybe they were goddesses. No one seemed to notice their state of undress.

Aurélie folded her arms and told herself if they didn't mind being here half naked she surely couldn't feel underdressed in faded jeans, boots and her favourite red turtleneck pullover. It was just that she was nervous, her heart beating high in her throat.

She wished she'd found time to change into her dress and heels. Her foot tapped nervously and a churning in her stomach spoke of fear.

Fear that, after coming all this way, she'd be fobbed off. Fear that there was no way of getting a private message to—

'Ms Balland?' A thin man in an impeccably cut suit emerged from a door in the gilded panelling.

Aurélie shot to her feet. 'Yes, that's me.'

'I'm sorry to keep you waiting. But I'm afraid your request is impossible. People don't walk into the palace unannounced and demand an appointment.'

'Request. I *requested* an appointment.'

'Nevertheless…'

'Believe me, if I'd been able to make an appointment in the normal way, I would have. I tried and every time was told it's impossible.' She heard her voice waver on the last word and swallowed hard. She wouldn't be put off this time.

The man smiled as if sympathising, but his eyes remained watchful. 'If you'd like to tell me why you believe you need this interview—'

'No!' Her voice rose and the security guard stirred as if expecting her to run amok. She took a deep breath, searching for calm, despite the unease feathering her spine and the queasy cramp of her belly.

'In that case, I'm afraid I can't assist you. But—' his raised hand forestalled her protest '—if you leave a note I'll see it's delivered.'

Aurélie was already shaking her head before he stopped talking. Any note would be opened and vetted by staff. 'This is a private matter.'

'Ah.'

To her surprise that one syllable sounded almost

understanding. She looked at the bureaucrat, only to find he wasn't watching her face but her hand, pressed low to her abdomen. Hastily Aurélie moved her arm to her side, heat flooding her cheeks as his gaze snapped to hers.

Suddenly, instead of feeling desperate and annoyed at the hurdles she faced, Aurélie felt vulnerable. And even more nervous.

Her breath came in shallow gasps. The cherubs above her seemed to tilt and she realised the chocolate bar she'd had on the bus was no substitute for a proper breakfast. Or lunch.

To her surprise the man said, 'Perhaps this one time I might venture to make an exception. Come with me, please.'

From the corner of her vision she saw the security guard's eyes widen. Then the grey-suited man scooped up her pack and led her into a part of the palace the public never saw.

Aurélie finally had what she needed—the chance of a face-to-face meeting.

Why did that make her feel as if she'd burned her bridges?

Lucien ignored the vibration of his phone in his pocket. Again.

Instead he watched Ilsa walk up the aisle towards him, as beautiful as ever in high heeled boots, tailored trousers and a top of muted gold that matched her hair. Late afternoon light angled through the cathedral's stained-glass windows, so that as she reached him she was bathed in jewel colours.

She met his stare and smiled briefly. Ilsa, the girl he'd known years before, had grown into a lovely woman. Poised, elegant and good-natured. No wonder Justin had been happy to make her his bride in a dynastic marriage.

Lucien wished he could be more enthusiastic now he'd reluctantly stepped into his cousin's shoes. For with Justin's death, Lucien had stepped not only into his shoes but his crown and all his obligations.

Including the promise to marry the Princess of Altbourg.

Surprisingly it was only Ilsa who'd questioned his willingness. Not because she'd loved Justin, but because she knew Lucien hadn't been raised, like Justin, to expect a marriage of convenience. She'd been one of the few who fully understood the seismic shift in his life, catapulted from private citizen to King in a single day. The only others who truly recognised that were Felix, his royal secretary, and a few close friends.

Lucien breathed deep, aware of the air shuddering into his tight lungs. Of his rigid spine and shoulders, the ache at the base of his skull.

'Excellent,' said the archbishop to Ilsa. 'Then your father will place your hand in His Majesty's.'

They stood together before the old man as he went through the ceremony, describing each detail, ensuring they understood not only the process but its significance.

As if they didn't both already know!

Everything was riding on this marriage. It would join their two countries. Another step on the road to finalising plans that had been in the making for almost twenty years. A step towards an exclusive economic and trade zone between their nations. A symbol of hope and renewal to a country still reeling from the loss of two much-loved royals.

It would change Lucien's life for ever.

There would be no divorce, no separation if he and Ilsa couldn't make their relationship work. It would work because they'd *make* it work. It was expected, necessary.

Lucien drew in a slow breath, inhaling the pungent scent of lilies massed beside the altar. A shiver rolled up his spine to curl around his neck.

The over-rich perfume reminded him of the double funeral here two months ago. Justin's coffin and Uncle Joseph's had rested where Lucien stood now. There'd been hothouse lilies then too, arrangements of foliage and flowers. Green and white for the royal house of Vallort.

'Your Majesty?'

He blinked and realised the archbishop was waiting for him. Beside him Ilsa wore a hint of a frown.

'I'm sorry. Would you mind repeating that?'

'I said, at that point you'll be able to kiss your bride.'

Lucien nodded. 'Good. I see. And then?'

The clergyman hurried on to describe the rest of the procedure. Leaving Lucien to ponder how doing what he knew to be right, because it was his duty, could feel so wrong.

He tried to imagine kissing the woman beside him and couldn't. As for taking her to bed...

His lungs clamped.

No matter how beautiful his fiancée, and how necessary this marriage, when he thought of being naked with a woman it was a woman with fiery hair and fascinating brown eyes.

Lucien was no fool. He knew these were natural reservations about a cold-blooded marriage of convenience. Until now his love-life had been anything but cold-blooded.

As for the way his thoughts kept returning to Aurélie, it was probably because she'd been there when he needed someone. When his world turned inside out and he'd felt helpless in the vortex of loss.

At last the archbishop finished and it was time to walk down the aisle. Once they reached the cathedral's massive doors the rehearsal would be over.

He couldn't wait. With a brief smile for his bride-to-be he hooked her hand over his arm and led her away, telling himself his qualms about marriage would settle.

In the shadows something caught his eye. Felix, his private secretary, stood there, face unreadable. Yet his stance, his very stillness, communicated a warning. Lucien had weathered the challenges of the past two months fairly well but he always felt he barely juggled the multitude of royal demands. Now he sensed a problem, his nape tingling in pre-sentiment.

They reached the front of the cathedral and Felix approached. The archbishop had followed them and Ilsa turned to him, listening to him reminisce about the last royal wedding held here.

'Felix.' Lucien beckoned. 'What is it?'

'Something you need to know about immediately.' Felix's voice dropped and Lucien saw his gaze flicker to their companions. 'You have a visitor. I thought it best not to leave her in the palace's public rooms. The fewer who know about her the better.'

'There's a woman to see me?' He caught Ilsa's curious glance and lowered his voice. 'I don't see the problem.'

Felix had been Uncle Joseph's secretary. Lucien had never seen him flustered or unable to deal with a problem.

'I couldn't leave her alone in an office with so many confidential records, but I didn't want to bring anyone in to stay with her in case they learned too much about her.' Felix cleared his throat. 'The young woman refuses to state her business. She says it's strictly for your ears only.'

Lucien raised his brows. Growing up in the

country's ruling family he knew they attracted their share of cranks and fantasists.

'Surely you can deal with her.'

Felix shook his head. 'You need to see her.' He drew a slow breath and leaned closer. 'If I'm not mistaken her health is…fragile. I brought her through the private passage and she's waiting in the anteroom.'

'She's *here*?'

Lucien shot a look towards a dark corner of the building. There was a small chamber, usually locked, and beyond that a private passage the royal family used to cross between the cathedral and the palace next door. As he looked the carved wooden door cracked open and he glimpsed a figure wearing dark trousers and a vibrant red top.

'Her name is—'

'Aurélie!' The name shot from Lucien like a bullet from a gun. His breath jammed in his lungs while his heart hammered.

The archbishop turned, and Ilsa too. The door swung shut, blocking out the woman who'd stood there. Lucien had only seen her for a second but couldn't mistake her, even if her hair looked muted in the dark shadows.

His heart pounded and the skin around his nape grew tight. 'What do you mean, she's unwell?'

Felix flashed him a warning glance then turned to answer a question from the archbishop.

'Lucien? What's wrong?' Ilsa moved closer, curious.

Lucien forced down his confusion and shock. 'I'm sorry, Ilsa. I didn't mean to startle you. Felix has an unexpected visitor he wants me to see. That's all.'

As he spoke, Lucien felt another frisson of warning. This time it skated the full length of his spine. Aurélie had understood that they'd only ever share a single night. What brought her here?

He put his hand to his fiancée's elbow, steering her towards the main entrance. 'What time is your appointment? Your car will be waiting.'

She surveyed him with clear eyes. He saw she was curious but Ilsa was too polite to probe. She glanced at her elegant gold watch. 'You're right. It's time I left.'

Minutes later, with Ilsa on her way to meet friends, and Felix steering the archbishop away with questions about the wedding, Lucien made for the royal antechamber.

Aurélie felt sick.

A different sort of sickness to the nausea she'd felt in the gilded palace. The royal secretary had offered her coffee and her stomach had rebelled at the smell. She'd only just made it to the bathroom in time, chalking up the experience to her first ever bout of morning sickness.

What a time to begin!

The. Worst. Possible. Time.

She'd felt shuddery and weak, and worried that he'd guessed the reason for her illness.

She gnawed her lip and paced the small room.

What she felt now wasn't morning sickness; this was distress.

Because she'd seen Lucien with his bride-to-be. Rehearsing their wedding.

The first time she'd peeped out of the door she'd seen the pair of them hand in hand before the altar. Lucien handsome in a dark suit and his fiancée stunningly beautiful with her poise, her gold hair and couture clothes.

Aurélie's palm slipped across her flat abdomen as if in reassurance that everything was okay.

But nothing was okay. Everything was topsy-turvy.

It had taken such courage to come here, seeking out Lucien. She hadn't expected to barge in on his wedding rehearsal!

Gingerly she sank onto a hard-backed chair as her knees began to wobble.

The last weeks had been one shock after another. She'd told herself everything would be okay. Billions of women faced pregnancy at some point.

But many of those had a supportive partner or family.

Aurélie had neither.

More, she was finally on the verge of achieving her dream of attending university. A goal fostered all those years ago by her mother who'd encouraged her to dream big. Now that looked like being put on hold, again. How could she move to the city, support herself and study full-time? Once the baby arrived…

The door swung open and there he was.

Lucien. Her one-night lover.

He looked different. Had he lost weight? Maybe it was seeing him in the exquisitely tailored suit, complete with mirror gloss shoes and a perfectly knotted crimson tie. His hair, which had been just a little over-long before—tempting her to run her fingers through it—was impeccably styled.

He looked like what he was. No longer her sexy stranger but the King of Vallort.

That had been another shock. She'd set about searching online for him, expecting it would be like looking for a needle in a haystack. Instead she'd had immediate success.

If you called it a success to discover the man you'd slept with was a king. And that he was about to marry another woman.

Aurélie got to her feet. 'Your Majesty.'

Something passed across his face. A ripple of emotion gone so quickly she couldn't identify it.

'It *is* you.' He didn't approach, but stood inside the door.

That was the instant Aurélie realised part of her, the part that had listened to fairy tales at her mother's knee, had imagined him striding across the small room and sweeping her into his arms.

Not that she expected a happy ever after. She was no Cinderella.

But they'd shared so much that night. The experience had been a shining beacon in a drab world of disappointment and dull, grey mundanity.

Now she realised the glow she felt whenever she recalled that night was one-sided. Judging by his grim mouth and furrowed brow, Lucien didn't share her fond memories. His jawline was sharply defined and his eyes…she couldn't remember his eyes looking so cold. Even when she'd found him half-frozen on the street. Then he'd looked blank and bewildered. Now he simply looked hard.

'Why are you here, Aurélie? What do you want?'

And hello to you too!

Okay, so a warm welcome wasn't on the cards. But did he need to sound so brusque?

Disappointment merged with outrage. Clearly her memories of their night together were rose-tinted. This was the real Lucien. The one she remembered was a mirage.

'I came to see you.' She found her hands twisting together in front of her and put them behind her back so he couldn't see them. 'We need to talk.'

'Are you all right? Felix thought you weren't well.'

Did that mean Lucien cared after all? Yet she

didn't feel that warmth of connection that had made that night so amazing.

Her breath eased out in a disappointed sigh.

'I'm fine.' Except that her life wasn't her own any more. Nor was her body. As for her long-delayed plans, they were dying before her eyes.

I'm scared. I'm totally out of my depth.

But looking up into that stern face, Aurélie would never admit that. Not to this man who was more a stranger than the Lucien she'd known in Annecy.

'Then why are you here? And now of all times?' That was when she heard it, a trace of anger.

She lifted her chin, refusing to let his temper daunt her. Her father and stepmother had treated her like a slave, hurling abuse if she didn't anticipate their needs. She would *not* be bullied by this man too.

'I didn't plan to arrive when you were...' Her throat constricted and she waved a hand in the direction of the aisle where he'd walked with his oh-so-suitable fiancée. 'Rehearsing for your wedding.'

One dark eyebrow arched and she was treated to a stare as supercilious as any she'd ever seen.

It was on the tip of her tongue to tell him she wasn't awed by royalty. France was a staunch republic and had guillotined one king.

'No?' The single syllable carried a weight of distrust.

'No!' She took a slow breath and sought calm.

'Can we sit?' She looked around at the couple of hard wooden chairs.

'I prefer to stand. I don't have much time. I'm needed elsewhere.'

It was probably true. Yet it sounded like a personal insult. As if she were some footnote in his personal history that he'd rather forget.

Which meant she probably had her answer already. It had been pointless coming here. But she needed to be certain.

Aurélie drew a deep breath. Telling herself it didn't matter that this man was royal. That she wasn't daunted by his fancy clothes or the fact she looked washed out and travel-weary in old jeans.

'I came all this way because something's happened.'

She faltered to a stop, horrified at how emotional she felt, sharing her news with an uncaring stranger. She swiped her tongue around her dry lips and forced herself to continue.

'I'm pregnant, Lucien. You're going to be a father.'

CHAPTER FOUR

LUCIEN HEARD THE words but couldn't process them.

Usually he was a quick thinker. In his architectural practice he coped easily with change, whether the result of difficult clients, challenging sites or his own inspiration. In the last couple of months he'd risen to one challenge after another, shedding his old life and acquiring responsibility for a kingdom.

Today he felt mired, his reactions slow.

Because the last time he'd set foot in here it had been to bury his family? Because he felt trapped in a nightmare?

But this was no dream. Aurélie was real.

Hungrily he ate up the sight of her with her vibrant hair and all that remembered softness beneath the bright red pullover. She was a burst of flame and heat in a world of chill bleakness.

He wanted to reach out and touch her. Haul her to him and keep her close, like a talisman, a reminder that there was light in the world.

'A father?' He shook his head.

Lucien understood the words but applying them to himself seemed impossible. It had been just one night.

One memorable night.

Brutally, he cut short the memories. He couldn't go there. Not when he had a fiancée, a whole nation, depending on him.

'You're sure?'

Lucien searched her face, finally noting her tension and her pallor. Initially all he'd registered was her miraculous presence. Then the bright colour she wore and that gorgeous hair.

And a tide of something that felt almost like relief, running hot through his belly.

The mouth he remembered as lush and soft flattened into a crooked line. 'You think I'd go to the trouble of locating you and come all this way if it wasn't true?'

'No.' It was there in her face. Aurélie wasn't lying.

An invisible fist punched him in the ribs, winding him.

Now Felix's words made sense. Beneath that feistiness she looked fragile. That hint of vulnerability scraped at his protective instincts.

'Sit down, please.' He gestured to the chair behind her.

'I thought you were in a rush?'

Lucien hadn't seen that proud, argumentative angle to her jaw before. Stupid to find it attractive, given the gravity of their situation. Yet he felt a tug of pleasure, deep in his belly, at the sight of her flashing stare and up-tilted chin.

Or maybe it was relief in recognising she wasn't as weak as he'd feared.

'You look like a strong breeze would knock you over. Sit, Aurélie. This is no time for pride.'

Lucien took a chair at right angles to hers. He saw pique war with weariness before she subsided onto the seat.

'Talk to me.'

She frowned. 'I've told you. I'm going to have a baby. There's nothing else to tell you.'

Of course there was. Lucien wanted to hear how she'd found out. How she felt about it. How she was faring.

Except she was right. He wasn't simply Lucien, talking to a one-time lover. He was a king faced with news that could wreak havoc in his kingdom. Like it or not he had other priorities he couldn't ignore.

'Have you been to a doctor? Had a test?'

'Yes and yes. I'm two months pregnant and so far everything is going normally.'

His gaze dropped to her bright red pullover. There was no sign of a bulge. But maybe it was too early for that. Lucien knew next to nothing about pregnant women.

Or babies.

Like a brick thrown through plate glass, reality smashed into him. In seven months there was going to be a living, breathing baby. A squirming, squalling bundle needing care and love. Not just in seven months but in all the years that followed.

Lucien sat back, his spine colliding with unyielding wood, his breath escaping in a whoosh of air.

'What's so funny?'

'Funny?' Then he realised his mouth had curled up at the edges. It must look to her like a smile but in fact it was a grimace of shock.

Was there anything else fate could throw at him?

He'd lost his family. The only people he truly loved in the world. He'd been forced to give up the career he'd worked so hard at and reinvent himself as a royal. He'd even agreed to take on a wife he didn't love in a marriage he didn't want.

Now it seemed he was going to be a father.

He shook his head. He doubted Aurélie would sympathise. She had her own problems.

'Nothing at all.' He drew a slow breath and fixed his gaze on hers. 'You say it's my baby?'

Her response was instant, as if a bolt of lightning shot through her. She stiffened, nostrils flaring and eyes narrowing. The hands in her lap clenched hard. 'I wouldn't be here if there was any doubt.'

It confirmed Lucien's instincts about her.

Yet, it pained him to admit it, his new position changed things.

Lucien the private individual might be satisfied with Aurélie's word, but now he was Lucien the leader of a nation, and he had a duty to be careful. Especially as he recalled his cousin Justin fielding two separate paternity claims from women who'd liked the idea of becoming Queen. One had been a complete stranger who'd never met Justin. The other an ex-lover whose baby was conceived months after they'd split.

'So you won't object to investigators looking into your recent past, to check for other lovers?'

Her warm brown eyes turned chilly and her skin seemed to shrink back against her bones, making her look starkly fragile.

'I do object but I suspect I have no choice if that's what you plan to do.'

Guilt eddied inside. But no matter his personal inclinations, Lucien had to do this. If he didn't, others would. He didn't want anyone else interrogating Aurélie.

'And you'll agree to a paternity test?'

She shot to her feet, pacing across the small space then spinning on the ball of her foot and stalking back to stand before him, hands on hips and breasts heaving as she struggled to contain her emotions.

She looked magnificent. An embodiment of pure energy. And, he admitted, spontaneous sexuality. A few strands of her glorious hair had escaped to frame her face. Her pallor was banished by a flush of what he guessed was fury and her eyes sparkled.

Lucien curled his hands into fists on his thighs as temptation assailed him. He wanted to touch her, try to connect with all that sizzle and snapping electricity.

'You're calling me a liar?'

Slowly he rose, still battling the urge to reach for her. To warm himself with her glowing heat.

To wrap his arms around her, seeking that sense of wondrous peace she'd given him.

Lucien shook his head. 'Put yourself in my position, Aurélie.' His voice bottomed out on her name, as if saying it scraped his senses raw. 'I'm a king. My children will stand in line to inherit a throne. I owe it to my people to be sure about this.'

Before his eyes she seemed to shrink in on herself. Her hands lifted to rub up and down her arms, as if warming herself against a sudden chill. Lucien hated that she felt that way because of him. Her spontaneity and generous warmth were so precious.

'And to your fiancée,' she reminded him.

Lucien's jaws clamped.

Ilsa. As if he needed reminding. How was he supposed to explain this to his bride-to-be?

For a moment he let himself wonder if this could be sufficient reason to cancel the royal wedding.

But this deal was bigger than either of them. It was about the future of their countries. Plans for this royal match were an unstoppable juggernaut. Even an unexpected baby wouldn't undo that.

'I won't do anything that might endanger the baby.' Aurélie folded her arms across her chest. 'If there's any risk at all to its health then you'll have to wait till after it's born to do your test.'

'Agreed.' Lucien knew nothing about how paternity tests worked but that was fair enough. He couldn't ask Aurélie to risk the baby's well-being.

'I didn't come to make trouble.' Her gaze held his

and this time the glacial chill was absent. 'I thought you had a right to know you're going to be a father.'

Her mouth crimped at the corners and pain sliced through Lucien. He'd barely had time to consider how much of a burden Aurélie was carrying.

'I understand.'

He didn't, of course. He was still processing her news, but it took no imagination to understand that however big a shock this was to him it must be more for the woman carrying his child.

His child.

Emotion sideswiped him. Aurélie was most likely carrying his baby. Once more his gaze swooped down to that flat belly behind the bright wool. He remembered kissing her there. The soft cushion of her skin fragrant beneath his cheek.

Arousal juddered through him, instantaneous and shockingly real, yanking him out of this cool little chamber and straight back to her bed.

'Please sit down, Aurélie. I meant it when I said you look unsteady on your feet.'

Slowly she subsided onto the hard chair. It struck him that he should take her somewhere more comfortable. Somewhere warm and cosy. But this place had one huge benefit. They'd be uninterrupted.

'What *did* you expect in coming here?' He knew it had been no small feat. How had she got past the royal minders to Felix?

'Sorry?'

'You said I had the right to know about the baby.

But what are your plans? What do you want, Aurélie?'

'You *do* think I came here to…what? Extort money from you?'

'I mean, do you want to keep the child?'

'Oh!' Her eyes rounded and one slim hand slid across her abdomen. It was such an inherently protective gesture and it told him so much about Aurélie.

Relief feathered the back of his neck. No matter how many complications a termination would remove.

'Yes, I think so.'

Think so? He sat straighter, every sense on alert. 'You're considering a termination?'

She shook her head and met his stare, her chin again taking on that determined cast. 'I know it might be simpler. Neither of us planned on a child. But I don't want a termination.' She paused and he felt the weight of her regard like a touch. 'It's crazy. I've never felt particularly maternal and I've already spent enough time looking after little kids. But, despite the burden, I don't feel comfortable just…ending this.'

'You see this baby as a burden?' It shouldn't surprise him. He wasn't the one who'd have to carry it then give birth to it, yet Lucien wanted his baby to be wanted. What future could it have with a woman who only grudgingly accepted it?

'Of course it's a burden.' Her eyes flashed. 'It

might be a miracle and if the mothers I know are to be believed, it could be the most wonderful thing in my life. But nothing is that straightforward. I have plans…*had* plans…and they don't include a child.' She spread her hands. 'I still need to think that through.'

'What sort of plans?' A man? Was that what she meant?

'To study. I've dreamed for so long about going to university and I won a place too. But I already had to defer my studies once to help my family.' She looked down at her hands, now pleating the edge of her pullover. 'It's important to me to better myself. It's what kept me going through…things. But how can I study and support myself and look after a child too? I'll be giving birth around the time the academic year starts.'

Her words reminded him how little he knew of Aurélie. Of her upbringing, her dreams and how it was that she'd spent time looking after young children.

'What about family support?'

Her mouth twisted. 'I'm on my own.'

No mistaking the finality of her tone.

'Then you came here so I can support you.'

Her head rocked back. 'I came here because I respected your need to know. I was acting responsibly. But now you mention it, would it be so wrong to expect my child's father to help out in caring for it?'

Lucien thought of all the press coverage there'd been of his engagement and approaching wedding. He thought of the huge disparity between his wealth, even before he'd inherited the throne, and a waitress's wages. Of her tiny apartment tucked in the eaves of an old building and his luxurious lifestyle.

Of course she'd come to him.

'So,' he murmured, 'after coming all this way, I assume you have a figure in mind?'

CHAPTER FIVE

AURÉLIE BENT AT the waist, hunching protectively as Lucien's words hit. They were bites against soft flesh, a tearing ache through her middle.

Her eyes snapped wide open and she saw her shock reflected back on his face, as if he too were taken aback by what he'd said.

He'd accused her of putting a price on her baby's head, coming to extort payment.

'Aurélie, that didn't come out right.'

She stumbled to her feet, ignoring his words. They seemed to come from a long distance, indistinguishable over the roaring blood in her ears.

Her lips twisted as the sour tang of disillusionment filled her mouth.

She'd thought better of Lucien. She'd imagined…

That was the problem. She'd imagined too much. He was simply a man who'd had no-strings-attached sex with her. Everything she thought she knew about him was suspect.

All she knew for sure was what he did and said. Today that wasn't edifying.

Aurélie swung round and wrenched open the door to the passage she'd followed from the palace.

An arm shot out in front of her, blocking her way.

She stared at the hand anchored on the doorjamb and remembered those long fingers caressing her, making her body thrum in pleasure.

Frantically she dragged in a deep breath, only to find it scented with something that reminded her of mountain forests and the sultry heat of sex.

'Wait, Aurélie. We need to talk.'

She surveyed the fine suit fabric of his sleeve in a designer shade of charcoal. The pristine white cuff, secured with a heavy cufflink. The watch that must have cost more than she'd earn as a waitress in a decade.

Everything reinforced the yawning gap between them. They were no longer equals. No matter what she did or said, Lucien would believe she wanted his money.

She should stay and negotiate a settlement because the baby would need it, given her meagre savings. But the voice of logic was drowned by pain.

Aurélie shuddered. 'We've talked.'

She needed somewhere to lick her wounds and think about what to do next.

Quickly she ducked, scooting under his imprisoning arm and into the flagstoned passage. Her breathing was raw, her lungs aching as she almost ran. From just behind came the sound of footsteps.

'Aurélie, please! At least slow down. These flagstones are uneven. You don't want to trip and injure yourself or the baby.'

That stopped her mid-stride. She flung her arm out to the panelled wall for support and drew a shuddering breath. In the light from the high windows she saw the worn stones were uneven.

It wasn't like her to panic, yet she felt that skittering sensation, the urge to flee.

Because she'd hoped Lucien would live up to the idea of him she'd built in her imagination. If he wasn't real then she was more alone than ever.

Aurélie dropped her hand from the wall.

She was stronger than that. She'd learned self-reliance long ago. She'd cope, no matter how overwhelming everything seemed.

Slowly she stepped forward, concentrating on putting one foot in front of the other, all the way back to the grand baroque palace where she'd felt so utterly out of place. But it wouldn't be for long. She'd grab her pack and go. She'd find a hostel for the night and tomorrow she'd leave.

A veneer of calm cloaked her as she walked. Even the sound of measured steps following didn't bother her. At least he didn't try to stop her. He must realise she'd had enough.

Through a massive panelled door that thankfully opened easily then right, left and right to the office where she'd left her pack.

All was quiet, even those following footsteps were muted as they passed onto golden-toned wooden floors then thick carpet.

Aurélie pushed open the final door with relief. She'd get her pack and…

Another door opened and there was the secretary, carrying a cafetière. The coffee aroma hit, rich and pungent. She spun on her heel, trying to hold down a rising tide of nausea.

Aurélie blundered into a hard body. Hard and warm. Hands gripped her elbows and she was encompassed by comforting heat. But not comforting enough to stop the sickness.

The secretary spoke from behind her. 'Let her go, Lucien. She's unwell.'

Thankfully those hands released her and she staggered to the now familiar bathroom. She barely had time to snick the lock before she was retching, succumbing to morning sickness.

Fifteen minutes later, Aurélie smoothed her hair, pulling it back into a fresh ponytail. She wished she had lipstick to give her face more colour, but she'd left her purse with her backpack.

What did it matter how she looked when she was leaving? There was no one here she wanted to impress. Yet she felt gauche. This was the second time she'd retreated to be comprehensively ill. She felt washed out and it was an effort to hide her weakness.

What happened to morning sickness being in the morning? She thought of tomorrow's bus ride back to France and winced. It could be very uncomfortable indeed.

Pulling her spine straight, she entered the office. The secretary wasn't there, nor, thankfully was his coffee.

Aurélie would almost rather have faced that

when her gaze caught on an intense amber stare that feathered memories through her mind and her body. As if she only had to meet Lucien's gaze to be swept back into the sensual world they'd shared.

She snapped her gaze towards the view of an inner courtyard beyond the desk.

'Do you feel any better?' Lucien sounded concerned. He probably wasn't used to women running from him.

'Thanks. I'm good.' For now. She had no idea if this afternoon's experience was typical of what she could expect. The thought was daunting. 'I need to collect my luggage.'

She looked to where she'd last seen it but Lucien gestured to another door. 'This way.'

Aurélie hesitated. She didn't want to prolong conversation with a man who thought she'd come to take his money. Indignation vied with tiredness.

She entered another office, larger, luxurious, yet clearly a place for serious work. There might be a floor-to-ceiling bookcase on one wall, and comfortable-looking leather sofas either side of a lovely crackling fire, but the mail trays on that big desk were full, and the ergonomic keyboard and sleek computer were all business.

'Please take a seat.'

She shook her head. 'I want my luggage. Then I'll go.'

From the corner of her eye she caught Lucien's

frustrated movement, raking his fingers through that impeccably cut dark hair.

'Please, Aurélie. Hear me out for five minutes. Then I promise I won't stand in your way.'

Belatedly she realised where she was. At the heart of the palace in the King's study. Who else would have an office three times the size of her flat?

She stiffened, ready to refuse. But what would that gain? Besides, Lucien wasn't ordering. He was asking.

Aurélie crossed the beautiful antique carpet and took the corner of a sofa by the fire. It felt like sinking into an embrace and she wondered how she'd find the energy to pull her weary bones away from such comfort and the fire's welcome heat.

It was only after she settled that she saw the plate of cracker biscuits on a side table with a glass of water.

'Firstly, I apologise.' He didn't sit but stood facing her, frowning. 'I insulted you and that wasn't called for. My choice of words was unfortunate.'

'You didn't realise what you were saying?' Aurélie didn't hide her sneer.

'I mean I thought it likely you'd need help. I didn't mean to sound accusing.'

He put his hand on the carved mantelpiece which, she realised, was a work of art, decorated with mountain deer and ibexes. A second later he dropped his arm and shoved his hands in his pockets, clearly ill at ease.

'But you're right.' His eyes met hers. 'If we were still just Aurélie and Lucien my reaction would be different.' His chest rose on a slow breath. 'But I'm not simply Lucien. I'm a monarch with a country depending on me. A fiancée due to marry me in a month.'

'And people want things from you.' Aurélie's voice sounded flat, matching her disappointment.

It was fine to feel insulted that he questioned her motives. Yet she could see his side of things. Not enough to ignore the insult, but enough to try to view this without emotion.

'It's fairer to say I have obligations to others. And I'm still learning to accommodate those.' His mouth tightened and Aurélie remembered how distressed he'd been that night in Annecy, filled with grief.

It was only later, when she'd identified him through press reports, that she'd learned how much Lucien had lost. First his uncle, King of Vallort, who'd raised him like a son after Lucien's parents died during his infancy. Then, a mere day later, in a terrible twist of fate, Lucien's cousin, the heir to the throne, had died when a rockfall hit his car on a private road outside the city.

In two days Lucien had lost his closest family.

He'd had to give up his architectural business and come home to Vallort. Taking the throne he'd never expected to inherit must feel like stepping into dead men's shoes. Men who, presumably, had been dear to him.

Looking at his clouded eyes and taut features, Aurélie knew she should cut him some slack. A man in his position would have to check the child was his. Naturally he'd wonder how much she wanted from him.

Yet distress lingered. Aurélie folded her arms across her chest, trying to hold it in.

'I'm not here to cause a scandal. I don't want to blackmail you or sell my story to the press.'

Lucien nodded. 'But you need my help.'

Did she? Aurélie knew that, come what may, she'd manage. She had too much fighting spirit not to do her best for this baby. Yet doing it on her own would be tough.

'How do *you* feel about the baby, Lucien?'

'Me?' His eyebrows rose as if the question took him by surprise. Had he been too caught up thinking about consequences to consider his feelings? Maybe he didn't have any. Maybe he only saw this unborn child as a problem to be dealt with.

A chill frosted Aurélie's bones, despite the nearby fire. She hunched against the deep cushions.

'You're going to be a father. You must feel something.' This time saying those words had the strangest effect, making it suddenly real. As if the evidence of her own body and the doctor's confirmation weren't enough. An image wavered in Aurélie's mind, of Lucien holding a baby close, his shoulders curved protectively around it. But she couldn't make out his expression. Was he looking tenderly at his child or wishing himself far away?

'I feel...' He paused and reached for the mantelpiece. Firelight cast his features into gold and shadows, highlighting grooves beside his mouth and the strong angle of his jaw. His shoulders rose in a fluid shrug. 'Stunned. Excited.' He paused. 'Nervous.'

He fixed her with a stare as bright as the flames and Aurélie felt relief and warmth pour through her. He wasn't unaffected. The weight pressing down on her lifted a little.

'In awe that you're carrying a new life inside you.' His gaze dropped to her midriff and again she felt it like a caress on bare skin. The sensation didn't seem maternal but sexual, snatching her breath. Desire for Lucien was *not* what she needed.

'Incredibly aware that I know nothing about raising babies.'

Aurélie almost said that was okay because she had experience. But that might imply she thought they'd raise their child together. Nothing was more unlikely.

Yet she had to know.

'Do you want to be involved? As a father?' That was why she'd come. To find out.

Lucien moved so swiftly he took her by surprise. One minute he was standing on the other side of the fireplace, looking brooding and thoughtful, the next he was hunkered before her, his hand capturing hers.

Aurélie concentrated on steadying her breathing, hoping her runaway pulse would ease before he noticed how he affected her. He shouldn't, not now, but—

'Of course! This is my *child*.' He paused and she saw a flicker of expression on his face that might even have been awe. His fingers tightened around hers. 'I'd never turn my back on my child, my family.'

She remembered those headlines about the double tragedy in Vallort. How Lucien had lost his remaining family.

Was that why he was so eager to marry his beautiful Princess? To start making a new one as soon as possible?

Was he in love?

Aurélie ignored the ache behind her ribs. It was none of her business.

Except it would be, if she shared her child with Lucien and his other children from a royal marriage. She tried to imagine ferrying their child between the palace and her flat in Annecy and failed. Besides, she wouldn't be there. She'd have to find a place more suited to raising a child. In her home town? Or would she find a way, somehow, to attend university?

It was too much to think about now. She felt so weary and so disturbed by this man who felt no qualms about holding her hand and invading her space.

Aurélie told herself she didn't want to feel his warmth or inhale that teasing hint of male skin scent. Yet she didn't disengage her hand.

'So, we'll have to work out a way for you to be involved.'

Because the traditional solution, marrying to provide a home for the child they were expecting, was out of the question. He was a king and she was a waitress. There was no question of a match between them, even without his aristocratic bride waiting in the wings.

'We'll find a way.' His hand squeezed hers. 'But not now. You're tired and you've had enough stress for one day.'

He drew her to her feet and Aurélie didn't resist. It was a welcome novelty to have someone concerned for her instead of expecting her to look after them.

She didn't even object when he kept hold of her hand, telling herself she simply found comfort in the touch of another person, after weeks of feeling incredibly alone, worrying how she was going to manage.

At least the nausea had subsided. Her knees were shaky but she'd be fine.

'I'll get my luggage and find a room for the night.' A glance at the window told her it was getting late. She had an impression of looming mountains shrouded in cloud. Spring in this Alpine kingdom was slow coming.

'It's taken care of. Come.' He stepped away, releasing her hand, and she bit down an instinctive objection. Not at someone booking a room, but because her hand felt empty without his.

That was a bad sign.

She followed him, rubbing her palms together, trying to obliterate the sense memory of his touch.

Five minutes later she was lost. Surely it didn't take this long to reach the palace entrance?

Lucien pushed open a door and invited her to precede him. Aurélie stopped in a high-ceilinged room, her breath catching.

It was glorious. The walls were cream but the curtains and upholstery on the antique furniture was a fresh lemon shade that made the heart lift. Vases filled with yellow primroses, snowdrops and blue forget-me-nots gave the elegant room a welcoming feel. Beyond the window was a view of charming old buildings in a range of pastel colours and, rising beyond them, the dark blue slope of a mountain.

'Lucien?'

She turned. His gaze fixed on hers. That stare was so intense the blood in her arteries slowed to a ponderous, thrumming pulse.

Then he moved into the room and the spell broke.

'You need somewhere to stay. The palace has hundreds of rooms so it makes sense to stay here.

Your luggage is in your room.' He gestured towards an open door which she assumed led to a bedroom.

Stay under Lucien's roof? In the palace?

His fiancée won't like this.

Aurélie felt sorry for the woman. For all of them. What a mess!

'Tomorrow we'll talk again, discuss some options.'

Slowly she nodded.

'I've organised a doctor to visit you tomorrow too. I know you've had someone confirm the pregnancy, but you should get that morning sickness checked. You seem very fragile.'

Aurélie didn't know whether to be warmed by his concern or worried that she looked so bad.

'Okay.' Truth be told, she'd be glad to talk to someone about the sudden nausea. She knew lots of women suffered with it but hadn't realised how debilitating it could be.

No doubt the doctor would talk to her about a paternity test and how safe it would be for the foetus. She could be sure it would all be very discreet. Presumably that was why Lucien had arranged for her to stay here.

The warmth she'd felt at his thoughtfulness faded.

'Excellent. I'll leave you to rest. A maid will be here soon to draw a bath or do whatever else you need. Tell her what you'd like and dinner will be brought.'

Aurélie nodded, fully understanding, at last, Lucien's generosity. She'd stay in the palace, where she'd have no chance to talk to anyone or arouse curiosity about her reason for visiting Vallort.

Because if that became known there would be a huge scandal.

CHAPTER SIX

'ILSA, I NEED to talk with you about the woman at the cathedral.'

His fiancée's blue gaze met his across the coffee table. 'Is she your girlfriend?'

'No.' Why did it feel like a betrayal to Aurélie to discuss that night? Ilsa was his fiancée. He owed her the truth. 'But we spent a night together.'

She showed no shock. Had she guessed? He'd seen her curious gaze on Aurélie this afternoon.

'Recently?' In other words—after their betrothal?

'Two months ago. The day I heard about Justin.' He paused, scraping his voice from where it stuck to the back of his throat. He'd stepped into his cousin's life, his home and duties, even his engagement, but sometimes even now the pang of loss threatened to undo Lucien. 'I was on my way back here when she and I met. Before our engagement. I didn't set out to betray you.'

Slowly Ilsa nodded. 'I didn't think you would, but this is a dynastic marriage, not a love match.' Her gaze didn't waver. 'So you're not in love with her?'

The word caught him by surprise.

He enjoyed the company of women but he'd never been in love.

His only experience of love wasn't romantic.

It was what he'd shared with his aunt and uncle, who'd been like parents, and Justin, as close as any brother could be.

Now he'd discovered how much love cost. An outsider might envy him, inheriting a kingdom and a glamorous bride. Yet Lucien had lived in shadow and pain since the news had broken.

Except once, he realised in shock. One bright spot when the pain hadn't gone away, but receded enough to be bearable.

With Aurélie…

'You can't fall in love in a night.' He swallowed hard. 'But you can make a baby.'

'Ah.' Ilsa put down her teacup and leaned back against the seat. 'I see. That…complicates things.'

Lucien felt a surge of relief that his fiancée wasn't the sort to indulge in recriminations.

'It does.' With Aurélie's news, everything had altered. *Again.* Once more his world rocked on its axis.

He tried once more to imagine his child, maybe with dark hair, or his height. But his brain refused to cooperate.

Yet he had no difficulty picturing Aurélie round with his child, glowing and maternal. He could even imagine her holding a swaddled baby, but further than that his imagination wouldn't go.

'And she…?'

'Aurélie.'

'Aurélie is going to have the baby?' Ilsa's tone was even, but Lucien saw her tension.

'She is, though she's not sure she's ready to be a mother.' As he didn't feel ready to be a father.

'And you want to be involved? Do you want to marry her?'

Lucien's mouth tightened. He didn't want to marry anyone. But he couldn't say that to Ilsa.

He'd been forced into their engagement by the weight of expectation. The match between the Princess of Altbourg and the King of Vallort had been long planned. The fact that there was a new king hadn't altered those plans.

As for marrying Aurélie... Lucien barely knew her.

Yet the moment he'd seen her today he'd felt that whump of sensation in his chest. The flare of heat he remembered from their night together. It was still there.

But it wasn't love. That was impossible on such a short acquaintance. It was physical attraction.

Lucien unclenched his hands and spread his fingers over his thighs.

The fact that he didn't feel any such reaction to his attractive fiancée told its own story. This royal marriage wasn't about sexual compatibility but duty.

Yet surely he had an obligation to his child? And if he were to imagine spending long winter nights sharing a bed with anyone, his thoughts strayed to—

Lucien pulled himself up. He didn't have the luxury of acting like a private citizen.

'I'm an engaged man and there's no easy way out of our wedding, is there, Ilsa?'

He watched her closely, alert to any sign that she too felt discomfort at what was expected of them. But Ilsa said nothing, silently reinforcing his words. They were both trapped. Lucien's mouth tightened.

'Aurélie and I have nothing in common except the baby she's going to have in seven months.'

Ilsa leaned forward. 'But you want to be involved with the child?'

He inclined his head. 'I'm sorry, Ilsa. I know I'm bringing trouble your way. There'll be gossip and scandal. But I can't walk away from my child.'

Lucien drew a deep breath and felt his tight lungs ease. Despite the consequences, this was one thing he knew for sure. One thing that felt *right*.

'The baby is my responsibility. I have a duty to be involved. I *want* to be involved.'

Lucien knew how important family was. His aunt and uncle had welcomed him into theirs when he was orphaned. He wouldn't be the man he was today but for them. His life could have been so different if he'd been fostered by someone unable to love him like a son.

'I could never shun my own child.'

'I understand.' Perhaps she did. Ilsa knew his history. Besides, she seemed a compassionate woman.

He reached for his coffee and took a sip, to discover it was cold. He put it down, remembering Aurélie's reaction when she'd smelled coffee.

Lucien stiffened, aware his thoughts had strayed. Though Ilsa seemed lost in her own thoughts too.

'The issue,' he said slowly, 'is what to do now.' Being engaged to one woman while having a baby with another would be complicated at the best of times. When he was a newly minted king trying to manage national and international expectations of a royal wedding…

'You say Aurélie doesn't feel ready for motherhood?'

He frowned. 'It's come as a surprise. She had other plans.'

'I'm not disapproving, Lucien, just making sure.' After a moment she sat forward, her forehead crinkling. 'Because I have an idea…'

Morning sun streaming through the windows washed Lucien in warm light as he crossed the sitting room. He wore another perfectly tailored suit. The sunlight caressed his chiselled jaw and the slight furrow along his brow, at odds with his smile of greeting.

Aurélie shifted restlessly on the sofa. Once Lucien had made her feel wonderful. Now his towering presence in the suite where she'd spent the night made her nervous.

Not because he was royal.

Because, despite telling herself yesterday's response to him was due to tiredness and stress, she still felt his sexual pull. Her hormones stirred.

He doesn't want you here. You're a problem to fix.

Her chest squeezed. She felt bereft, knowing they were no longer equals. She yearned for the man he'd been two months ago. An amazing, generous lover who'd made her feel cherished.

'How are you feeling today, Aurélie?'

'Better, thank you. I've been very comfortable.'

That was an out-and-out lie. She'd occupied a grand half-tester bed in a room filled with antiques that looked as if they belonged in a museum. Years before she'd visited the palace at Versailles on an excursion and this place had a similar feel. Aurélie hadn't dared touch the furnishings, afraid she'd damage something priceless. She felt overawed.

At least she'd managed to keep her breakfast down and, despite her imposing surroundings, felt more rested than she had in weeks. She'd been working extra shifts, saving as much as possible for the future. An early night had been a welcome luxury.

'Excellent.' Lucien sat opposite her, his long legs stretched out. He looked relaxed in this stultifying opulence. As if ornately frescoed ceilings, gilt-edged furniture and the do-not-touch air of refinement didn't intimidate him. 'I was worried about you.'

Aurélie's heart jumped. 'You were?'

Their eyes met and she felt a little stab of sensation. It ran straight through her middle, warming her deep, deep inside. She stared into eyes the colour of amber and imagined heat there.

Imagined. To Lucien she was an unwanted complication. What they'd shared in Annecy was over, for him at least.

He frowned. 'You doubt it?'

'I…no.' Of course Lucien cared. He wasn't an ogre. Even if he hadn't been at his best yesterday.

'I asked the doctor to check on you today.'

'She's already been.' Aurélie had been glad to see a female doctor. Had Lucien arranged that specifically? 'She says I'm doing well.'

'And that you need rest.'

Slowly she nodded. 'She said I should try to avoid stress.'

Lucien's eyebrows rose and a wry smile curved his mouth. For a second it felt as if they shared silent camaraderie. As if stress could be avoided in these circumstances!

An answering smile tugged Aurélie's lips. The moment strung out between them, neither moving. It could only have lasted seconds yet to Aurélie's fertile imagination it seemed as if neither wanted to shatter the connection.

Her thoughts moved to what else she'd discussed

with the doctor. The non-invasive paternity test using blood drawn from the mother and a mouth swab from the father. Learning there would be no danger to the baby, Aurélie had asked the doctor to take blood from her arm right away. The sooner Lucien knew the baby was his, the better.

Yet the thought of needing to prove her child's paternity brought her back to reality. This wasn't the sort of relationship she wanted with a man. Where was the trust?

But you're not beginning a relationship with Lucien.

'It would be best if you stayed here.'

'Sorry?'

'I'd like you to stay, as my guest, till you feel better. And till we agree on what we'll do about the baby.'

That was the nub of it—the baby. Lucien might be caring but she wasn't his main concern. What was?

The baby they'd made?

Avoiding scandal?

Pleasing his fiancée?

Aurélie's mouth dried and nausea stirred. She reached for her glass of water, taking a sip, telling herself the sudden discomfort could be dealt with by mind over matter.

'You're sure you're all right?' Lucien leaned in, elbows on his knees.

Aurélie smiled, willing her mouth not to wobble. See, she was fine.

'Yes. Nothing to worry about.' She took another sip of water.

Lucien sat back and she had the impression of energy fiercely leashed. He was waiting for something.

'You came to talk to me.'

'It can wait till you're feeling better. I can see you're not quite yourself.'

Aurélie couldn't help it. She laughed, the sound half amused, half bitter.

'You might have a long wait. I haven't felt normal for a long time.' Even before the morning sickness there'd been a sense of unreality as she'd tried to come to grips with news of her pregnancy. 'I've got seven months to go.'

Then the changes would really begin. Aurélie would be a single mother. The only thing she knew for sure about the future was that she and Lucien wouldn't be playing happy families together.

He scowled. 'The doctor said you'd be sick for the rest of your pregnancy?'

Aurélie stared at his outraged expression. Stupidly, that warmed her lonely heart. 'No. She said it happens very occasionally but it's highly unlikely. She's given me some tips for managing it.' She glanced at the plate of biscuits beside her glass. Smaller, more frequent snacks had been one suggestion.

'You need looking after.'

'I'm not an invalid.' Aurélie wasn't sure whether she was trying to convince Lucien or herself. She'd been shocked at how bad she'd felt yesterday, but the doctor had suggested overwork, travel and stress might be factors. 'What did you want to discuss?'

As if she didn't know. Her fingers tightened on her glass.

'The future. Our child.'

Our child.

Surely it was pregnancy hormones that made those two words sound intimate. As if she and Lucien were embarking on this together, like a couple.

'Does your fiancée know?'

He nodded. 'I told her last night.'

Aurélie's eyes rounded. 'And you still want me to stay here? That doesn't seem right.' How must the Princess feel, learning her husband-to-be was about to become a father with another woman?

It struck her that *she* was the 'other woman' in this triangle.

Her breath became a hiss of shock and she rubbed her forehead with her fingertips. This was such a mess.

'Aurélie, it's okay.' Lucien half rose as if to touch her but she shrank back in her seat.

She didn't want his touch. Yesterday had proved that she was anything but immune to him. He'd taken her hand and ignited a longing that she couldn't—wouldn't—allow herself to feel. Her only hope was to keep her distance.

Warily she watched him frown then sink back into his seat. His jaw clenched and a tiny muscle worked there as if tension rode him hard. Aurélie wanted to reach for him, feel the clasp of his hand. Instead she stiffened her spine.

'Ilsa is reasonable. Fortunately she's not prone to panic or outrage.'

His mouth curved in a tight smile and Aurélie felt pain jab her ribs. Surely that wasn't a stab of jealousy?

'You mean she doesn't *mind* that you've got a pregnant ex-lover?' The words emerged sharply, like an accusation, and she pressed her lips together. She shook her head. 'Sorry. I didn't mean to sound—'

'Ilsa is a remarkable woman,' he said stonily and Aurélie felt about an inch tall.

What was wrong with her? The Princess hadn't done anything to her. Aurélie had never expected a permanent relationship with Lucien, even before she'd realised his royal status.

'I'm sure she is.' That spike of discomfort jabbed again. Aurélie told herself indigestion was a well-known symptom of pregnancy. She was *not* envious. She wasn't looking for Prince Charming.

Lucien scrutinised her and Aurélie once more felt that prickly sensation sweep across her skin. Like an electrical charge that made the hairs on her arms stand up. She had the uncomfortable idea that he read her jumbled emotions whereas she had no idea what went on in his head. His expression was unreadable.

'Ours isn't a love match.'

Aurélie opened her mouth to ask if that meant they wouldn't be faithful, then, horrified, snapped it shut. It was no business of hers.

So why did she feel a rush of relief?

'I explained we'd been together before she and I became engaged.'

Aurélie nodded. When she'd discovered who Lucien was she'd been horrified to learn he was engaged, wondering if she'd been a passing amusement for a man already tied to another woman.

It hadn't fitted with what she knew of him but she wouldn't have been the first woman fooled by a guy. It had been a relief when she'd discovered their engagement happened after he'd returned to Vallort.

'The engagement still stands? She hasn't been frightened off?' Aurélie watched for some clue to his feelings.

Lucien shook his head and Aurélie felt something within her dip.

'Too much rides on our marriage for us to back out. Negotiations between our countries have taken years.'

That didn't sound like a good basis for a marriage but what did she know? When she was little she'd had a romantic view of love and marriage, inherited from her mother. Watching her father marry a scant six months after her mother's death, and to a woman like her stepmother, had dashed Aurélie's illusions. Her cosy belief that her father had unwaveringly loved his first wife was long gone.

Reality had cured Aurélie of romantic dreams.

'I see.' She nodded as if she really did understand how two people could marry for reasons that had nothing to do with personal preference. But perhaps that *was* a factor. Princess Ilsa was beautiful. Maybe Lucien *wanted* to marry her. Maybe they were lovers.

That sick feeling stirred anew in her stomach.

'Meanwhile we need to decide what to do about the baby.'

As if it were an item to be ticked off an agenda.

Aurélie's hackles rose and she bit down a retort. She was being too sensitive.

Her hand slipped across her stomach in a gesture that was as much about comfort as protectiveness. Silently she vowed, again, to do the very best for her child.

'You've had an idea about that, have you, Lucien?' It felt bold and a little provocative, using his first name now that he was a monarch, but it made her feel more in control.

He shrugged, but the set of those wide shoulders betrayed tension.

'There are several options.' Their eyes met and

she felt he tried to gauge her mood. 'Especially since you said you weren't thrilled at the prospect of being a mother.'

'I...' She shook her head. There was no point feeling defensive or guilty. It was true.

She wanted the best for her baby. Yet she felt trapped, knowing it would change her life.

Aurélie had spent years as the primary carer of her younger half-brothers. She'd even postponed her studies when her father and stepmother played the guilt card, saying they'd never cope without her help while the last two were so young.

Was it any wonder she felt cornered, knowing what raising a child involved? Aurélie told herself she wouldn't turn bitter or resentful that her child would prevent her achieving her dream of study and a better future when she'd finally come so close to achieving it.

Yet doubt niggled that maybe she *would* grow bitter. That scared her. She wanted her child to have love and positivity in its life. Not constant complaints and blame, as Aurélie had experienced after her mother had died. Nor the scrimping for money that made life tough when there wasn't enough love.

'I said yesterday that I want to be an involved father. That hasn't changed.'

Something inside eased at his words. 'I'm glad. It will be better for our baby.'

Abruptly Lucien's gaze dropped to her mouth,

making Aurélie hyper-aware of the way her lips shaped the words. Warmth trickled through her as she looked into eyes like flame and felt that flicker of connection again.

She sucked in air. 'What are you thinking? Visits to France? Sharing care?'

'Both those are possible.' Lucien hooked his finger around his tie and loosened it. 'There's a third option too.'

'There is?' Aurélie had been around the issue so many times but hadn't come up with an alternative, apart from the obvious—bringing up the baby alone.

'Yes.' He paused, eyes watchful. 'If you don't want to raise the child, Ilsa and I could adopt it, make it our legal heir and bring it up in Vallort.'

CHAPTER SEVEN

'You *what*?' She couldn't have heard right. Except she had. 'You want me to give my baby to you and your…wife—' a knot in her throat threatened to choke her '—and walk away?'

Aurélie shot to her feet to stand, trembling. Looking down at the man who surveyed her with watchful eyes.

Gone was the latent hint of nausea. Gone the fog that impeded her thoughts when she tried to imagine the future.

Instead, she saw everything with crystalline clarity. King Lucien and Queen Ilsa, beautiful, charismatic and gracious, waving from a royal balcony to an adoring crowd, holding *her* baby.

A toddler, taking its first steps across a polished palace floor into the arms of its smiling blonde mother.

A little girl, her fiery hair tamed into neat plaits, being sent away to an exclusive boarding school where she'd learn all the things expected of an aristocrat.

The images flashed through Aurélie's mind in an instant, alarmingly vivid. Pain banded her chest and she realised she'd forgotten to breathe. She inhaled quickly, dragging air deep into her lungs. Yet still her pulse thundered.

'Aurélie.' She blinked, focusing on that deep

voice, and saw Lucien on his feet. 'Please be calm and hear me out.'

'Calm?' She heard her voice turn shrill and swallowed.

'No one's asking you to walk away from your child.'

'That's how it sounds.'

The result was a sharp insight into her feelings for her unborn child. She'd thought herself tired of playing mother to her half-brothers and shouldering the maternal responsibilities her stepmother wouldn't. She might be frustrated and, yes, sad that once more her own plans for the future were disrupted. But she couldn't imagine turning her back on her baby and not seeing it again.

The idea constricted her breathing all over again.

'I'm sorry. I didn't mean to upset you. I should have explained better.'

'Oh, I understand.' Aurélie wrapped her arms around her middle in a gesture that was half protective, half defiant. 'Adopting my baby and raising it without me is pretty clear.'

Lucien stepped into her personal space, filling her field of vision, forcing her to focus on him and not the images in her head. Was that concern she read in his face?

'Adopting the baby so that it has every protection under our law and every right to inherit. That's a positive, surely?'

Aurélie blinked, running through his words.

She wasn't worried about inheritance; she was still coming to grips with adoption. 'Your wife would be its mother, not me.'

A shuddering began deep inside. Again she was stunned by how much the idea hurt.

Warmth closed around her upper arm. She felt the weight of Lucien's hand. Her nostrils flared as she caught a hint of scent, male flesh and mountain forests that dragged her back to that night in Annecy.

Her mouth tightened at the corners as she bit back words. Whether to demand he release her or ask him to hold her close, she didn't know. Being near Lucien aroused feelings that yanked her in opposing directions and made her feel totally vulnerable.

Because he isn't and never could be yours. He has a fiancée. A beautiful, glamorous fiancée who belongs in this world of royalty and privilege. A woman who's everything you're not.

'No one is going to take your child from you. This is just an option to consider.'

She wished she could believe him.

Once she'd believed in her father, trusted him, and that trust had been misplaced. He wasn't the man she'd once thought him.

'You can let me go now.' Maybe then she could think. How was it that his touch, his proximity, addled her thoughts?

For a heartbeat longer he held her, his bright gaze

snaring hers. He was so close his slow exhalation stroked her cheeks, sending a quiver of need humming through her.

Abruptly he stepped back, frowning, his hand falling. Yet to her disordered mind even that felt like a caress. As if he didn't want to let go, his fingers clinging as long as possible.

Fury rose at her capacity for self-delusion. Lucien was more than over her. He'd moved on to a woman he wanted in his life permanently. Aurélie had been okay for a one-night stand but that was all.

At least anger didn't make her weak.

'If you adopt the baby your wife will be its mother. You'll bring it up here and I'll never see it.' An aching emptiness carved through her middle.

Lucien shook his head. 'I can see you're upset, Aurélie, and I understand the idea must seem shocking. But give us some credit. You said you weren't sure you wanted to raise the child. This *suggestion*—' he emphasised the word '—arose from that possibility. It provides legal security, and a single stable home if you choose to give it up. Neither of us would stop you visiting whenever you want.'

But she'd be an outsider. An occasional visitor. Not a parent.

'It's only one option,' he added.

'But it's the one you want.'

He shrugged, his hands spreading. 'How about we sit down to discuss it? You still look far too pale.'

Aurélie disliked being an object of pity, or knowing she looked unwell. At the same time, Lucien's concern felt special. When she'd lived with her family, no one had worried about her well-being. She'd been the one to look after everyone else. Even when she'd been exhausted from overwork there'd always been someone demanding more.

She took her seat and watched him do the same.

'Aurélie, whatever we do has to suit all of us. This option would give our baby legal protection. It would mean that he or she would grow up in Vallort, used to palace life, which is vital if he or she is to have a royal role. But neither I nor Ilsa would bar you from contact.'

'You really think your fiancée would agree to bring up someone else's baby?'

'She's already said she would.'

Stupid to feel betrayed that he'd discussed this with the Princess. She wanted to say that this baby was her personal business—hers and Lucien's. But that would be childish. There were wider implications, even if it did feel as if she were already being replaced by another woman.

Aurélie fought to repress raging misery and think logically. Instead of smarting because Lucien had discussed her private business, she should be impressed at his honesty. Some men would conceal an illegitimate child, especially when they were marrying someone else.

'She's trying to please you. She'll feel different

when you have children together. Won't she want her children to take precedence in inheriting?'

Lucien shook his head, his gaze leaving hers as if his thoughts were on the Princess, not her. 'No. She's more than happy to do this.'

Which seemed unusual. Surely a royal princess would be concerned about precedence in the line of succession?

Lucien continued before she could press the point. 'I believe she'd be a good mother. Ilsa is kind and sensible.'

Was it Aurélie's overactive imagination or did that sound like faint praise? Surely a man should be more enthusiastic about the woman he was about to marry?

Not that there was anything wrong with kind and sensible. They were important qualities in a mother.

Aurélie told herself she was clutching at straws, trying to pretend Lucien didn't care for his princess bride. How pathetic was that?

'Your idea is that you and… Ilsa—' silly how tough it was to say her name '—would raise one big happy family? With my baby and any others you have brought up together?'

Lucien caught the doubt in her voice. More—cynicism.

'You don't believe I'm serious? Why would I lie?'

He'd known this discussion would be difficult. Naturally Aurélie had strong feelings about her child. Yet he wasn't used to people questioning his word. He sat straighter, jaw tightening.

Lucien had felt unprepared to become King, but he knew his duty and did it to the best of his ability. Now he felt stuck in a quagmire; whichever direction he went there were complications. Surely Aurélie could see he was trying to find a solution for all of them? That he was doing his best in difficult circumstances?

She must know he'd never deliberately hurt her.

Managing the fallout from this would be diabolically difficult but he was trying to protect Aurélie and the child.

Brown eyes fixed on his and the expression in them sliced the edge off his annoyance. It wasn't the look of someone being deliberately offensive. He saw sadness there. Sadness and disquiet. It stifled his indignation.

'I don't think you're lying. But you don't have any idea what the future might hold for this ideal family unit you imagine.' Aurélie's voice grew huskier and he had the strangest sensation, as if her words raked through him.

'And you do? You think you can see into the future?'

Her shoulders lifted in a tight shrug. 'I can tell you stepchildren aren't always welcome. Or welcome only on certain terms.'

Everything, from Aurélie's tone to her expression and tense body language, told him she meant it.

And that this wasn't only about their unborn child. The air seemed to thicken as she spoke. The way she sat higher indicated defensiveness. He leaned forward, sensing this was vital.

'You need to explain.'

Her eyes flashed. Impatience? Anger? But Lucien refused to put words into her mouth. He waited.

Finally she continued, her voice clipped. 'I thought it was obvious. Not all stepchildren are loved like the rest of the family. Love, approval, even a place in the family home can be conditional on...' she paused and waved one hand '...good behaviour.'

'You think we'd discipline this child more harshly than any others?' Lucien was still coming to grips with the reality of *this* baby, let alone others.

'It's not just about discipline but belonging.' He watched her hands clasp, fingers knotting as she moved to the very edge of the sofa. 'Being cared for rather than being seen as a burden or another pair of hands to help with chores.'

Something shifted in Lucien's chest. They'd gone from talking about theoretical future children to something quite specific.

'Is that what happened to you?'

Aurélie's eyes held his for a long moment. Then she turned towards the window.

'Weren't you welcome in your family?' Lucien saw her mouth tighten and regretted the need to push. But he had to know. For the sake of the child they were going to have.

And because he wanted to understand Aurélie.

The suffering he'd glimpsed on her face affected him. He didn't like seeing the resignation that came with long-standing, deep-seated pain. He forced himself to sit still, pushing his hands into his trouser pockets instead of rising and taking a seat beside her.

She shrugged again. 'My mother died when I was seven. Within months my father married again.' Her mouth turned down. 'My stepmother wasn't cruel and didn't beat me. But from the day of their marriage I never felt loved. Not by my father or my stepmother.'

Grave brown eyes met his. Instead of seeking sympathy, that stare felt challenging.

'I have three younger half-brothers, so I know about being part of a blended family. But my reality was different to your theory.' Her nostrils flared in distaste.

'You weren't happy?' That was obvious.

'I'd been loved, you see. My mother truly loved me.' Her lips curved in a wistful smile that faded almost before it formed. 'So I felt the loss when it wasn't there.' She shrugged and looked at her pleating fingers. 'Lots of older siblings look after the younger ones, so I wasn't special in that. But I was never allowed to feel part of the family like before.

I was the unpaid help, the one to do all the chores and take the blame when things went wrong.'

Lucien frowned. 'What about your father?'

'He took his cue from my stepmother. I was treated like a servant, abused if all the work wasn't done. Ignored otherwise. The boys picked up their attitude.'

Distaste soured Lucien's mouth. He was about to say that her brothers should have learned better. But Aurélie continued.

'I'm not afraid of hard work. But when it's clear your value is *only* because of that, not because of any intrinsic worth of your own, family doesn't mean the same.' Her mouth twisted. 'I delayed starting university because they said they needed me, that they couldn't manage without me. But three months ago, when my father inherited a smallholding on the other side of the country, they packed up and left without even asking if I wanted to go too.'

He was horrified. 'I'm sorry, Aurélie.'

'It doesn't matter. It's in the past.'

Was it? She still bore scars from her family's treatment. How much of her cheerful, friendly demeanour in the restaurant was real and how much a façade? Or, if not a façade, merely one side of a complex whole?

Lucien would give a lot to meet her so-called family and give them a piece of his mind.

He wanted to comfort her, draw her close and

tell her she *was* special. That she deserved to be cherished.

But he didn't have the right.

The knowledge was a slam of pain that reverberated through his chest and down to his churning belly.

'Of course it matters.' He watched her eyes widen and her mouth gape in surprise. 'Every child deserves love and support. I know that more than most, which is why I swear to you that, however we decide to bring up our baby, I'll do my best for it, and for you.'

'I… Good.'

She nodded, a jerky movement that made him wonder if she wasn't used to people supporting her. Surely, even if her family had failed her, she'd had friends, lovers—someone to fill that gap?

'I come to this from the opposite side,' he said.

'Sorry?'

'I didn't have step-parents but I was adopted. You know the story?'

'I read that your parents died when you were a baby.'

Lucien nodded. 'I don't remember them. All I knew was my adoptive family, my aunt, uncle and cousin. I knew they weren't my birth parents and that Justin was my cousin, not my brother.' He ignored the gravel roughness that tinged his voice as he mentioned them. 'But I never felt anything but loved. Justin and I received the same care and discipline. I never, for one moment, felt I didn't belong.'

'You were very lucky.' A gentle smile lightened Aurélie's features and Lucien felt another pang at the yearning he read there.

'I was.' His mouth curved in a crooked smile. All that he did now, accepting the throne and an arranged marriage, was tied to the love his family had given him. The desire not to let them down but to shoulder the responsibilities they'd left him and live up to expectations.

Though he'd never wanted a royal future. More than ever, it felt like a trap he couldn't escape.

'So.' She exhaled on the word. 'You're serious about this?'

'It's a good option. If you decide you don't want to bring up our baby.'

It struck Lucien forcibly that in other circumstances he'd offer to live with Aurélie to raise their baby together. Shotgun weddings might be old-fashioned but he preferred the idea of his child being born to his wife and having his name.

If he were still an architect and able to please himself, that was what he'd do.

It was easy to imagine being with Aurélie and their baby. Telling her about his day and asking about hers. Spending each night with her in his arms, her bright hair a halo on the pillow, those soft brown eyes welcoming him when he sank into her body and—

'But surely…' Her words dragged him to the present. 'Surely it's not so easy? You can't keep this secret.'

'Of course not.'

'But what about public opinion? And the press? If anyone discovers the baby is mine and not…your wife's, won't there be scandal?'

His lips curved in a tight smile. 'Of course it will be newsworthy.' Royalty might have its perks but it had its downside too. Press interest being part of that.

'There will be a flurry of interest whatever we do.' Lucien saw her eyes widen in horror and was glad he'd downplayed the inevitable fallout. 'But I'll help you. My staff will work with you. You won't be alone.'

Yet what if she decided to go it alone, returning to France as a single mother? Even with his support it would be tough.

'Surely adopting our baby, making it your heir, would create scandal in Vallort? Would people accept it?'

Lucien's mouth firmed. She was right. It wouldn't be a ripple of interest; it would be a furore. But he'd accepted the burden of kingship and was determined that, in this at least, tradition would bend to *his* demands.

'I told you I'll acknowledge my child. I won't walk away from that. This baby is my family, my flesh and blood. Nothing will make me turn my back on it.'

No matter what it cost him.

He breathed deep, turning his thoughts from the inevitable fallout to the worried woman before him. She looked drawn by strain.

'I've given you enough to think about. I'll leave you to rest.' Lucien stood. 'At the very least you should stay here until we agree what to do.'

The thought of her leaving, drifting off to some hotel where there was no one to look after her or, worse, getting on a bus back home, sent a shiver of dismay down his spine.

He needed her here. Because they had decisions to make. But mainly because she needed rest and care.

No matter what his secretary or anyone else said about keeping his pregnant ex-lover under the same roof as his visiting fiancée. What mattered most was here in this room. His unborn child and a woman who, whether she realised it or not, needed him.

Her chin lifted and their eyes met. Again he felt that disturbing frisson of response shudder through his body.

'I'll stay for now.'

Lucien wanted to push for more but he read obstinacy as well as tiredness in that pretty face.

He nodded. That would have to do for the moment.

CHAPTER EIGHT

AURÉLIE LOOKED DOWN the pedestrian street towards the sunlit mountains. In the last three days spring had arrived in Vallort. She felt its warmth and smelled it on the air.

Which made a nice change now her sense of smell seemed so heightened. Walking past a café and inhaling the rich coffee aroma made her nauseous, as did cigarette smoke.

She sat on a bench beside a planter box of budding flowers. In a few days it would be full of blooms.

Would she be here then?

She had to make a decision. Soon.

For her baby's sake and her own.

A woman could get used to living in luxury. More worryingly, seeing Lucien every day, however briefly, undermined her resolve to ignore her attraction. It tugged stronger than ever, despite discovering his royal identity.

Despite discovering he was almost married.

She sucked in a ragged breath and buried her hands in her pockets. It wasn't like her to dither over a decision. But she'd never faced one like this.

As well as suggesting adoption, Lucien offered money to support her through her pregnancy and beyond, whether or not she kept the baby. She could find a place near the university while she studied psychology. Lucien was generous. She'd have enough to cover childcare. But did she want that? Someone else caring for her baby while she studied?

Was she crazy to hesitate? She could achieve her goal of a university qualification and keep her child. But, even with support, Aurélie had no illusions that being a single mother would be easy.

Would her baby thrive better living with Lucien and Ilsa? Everything within her had rebelled at the idea. Until Ilsa had sought her out.

Instead of a cool, distant woman she could dislike, Aurélie had discovered the Princess to be genuine and likeable. Ilsa had disarmed her by admitting she thought Aurélie might be offended by the suggestion they adopt her child. She was right. Aurélie had been offended and hurt. Then Ilsa explained she'd recently received medical advice that, though she wasn't infertile, she had a condition which made pregnancy more difficult.

'Lucien didn't tell you, did he?' she'd asked and Aurélie had shaken her head.

'I thought not.' The Princess had stared at her stunning sapphire engagement ring. 'He's a decent man. He knows it's something I prefer to keep private.'

'I won't tell a soul,' Aurélie had assured her.

Ilsa had nodded. 'But you deserve to know.' She'd paused. 'I wouldn't marry Lucien if I were barren, because he needs heirs. But conceiving won't necessarily be easy. Which means if we *did* adopt your baby it would be a blessing, not a burden.' Her gaze had caught Aurélie's. 'The decision is yours, but I want you to know that. If you imagined I'd resent the child, you couldn't be more wrong.'

Aurélie sighed and stretched out her feet on the cobblestones. Where did that leave her?

Lucien had even suggested she enrol at university in Vallort so they could both be near their child.

Most men in his position would try to hide a child born in such circumstances, and its mother. But whenever Aurélie mentioned the scandal Lucien would face, adopting the baby or simply acknowledging it, he turned stubborn. He'd given up his own life to become King, he said, and the world would have to take him and his family as they were.

His family.

Aurélie strove not to read too much into that word. Yet it weakened her defences against him. She sensed that, whatever happened, Lucien would stand by their child. What more could she ask?

He and his fiancée were incredibly accommodating. Yet she couldn't bring herself to agree to adoption. At the same time the idea of being a single mother with no family support was scary. Her mouth flattened as she imagined asking for help from her father or stepmother. That would be futile.

Tired of her circling thoughts, she got up and strolled down the street. A drift of music reached her and she saw buskers in the distance, collecting a smiling crowd.

On both sides old buildings housed beautiful shops that vied with each other to create tempting window displays. From a patisserie with a display of mouth-watering pastries and cakes to boutiques of fabulous fashion and exclusive leather goods that reminded her Vallort was a wealthy, if small nation.

Yet the city had an attractive quaintness. Outside each shop the cobblestone pavement contained a mosaic of white stones. There was a mosaic design of glasses set in the cobbles outside an optician's. A stiletto heel in front of a shoe shop. Crossed skis on the ground outside a ski store and a scatter of coins outside a bank.

She smiled, lingering before a shop full of hand-made wooden toys, for which Vallort was famous. Then a bookstore with a display of bright children's books.

Aurélie imagined reading to her son or daughter before bed, as her mother had read to her every night.

Did she want to miss out on that? On holding her baby and watching it grow?

On the other hand, if she gave it up, it would be heir to a kingdom. Lucien had explained that her child would inherit if adopted or born in wedlock. It would have everything money could buy. Was she selfish to hesitate?

To her horror, tears pricked her eyes. No matter

what she decided, she'd wonder if she'd done right. All she could do was go with her heart.

Aurélie spun round and turned towards the palace.

'So, I've decided.' Aurélie frowned and looked at the fire crackling in the grate. The light played across her face, highlighting the intriguing curves and hollows of her features and the tension imprinted there. 'I'll keep the baby with me and go back to France. But you can see it whenever you want. Later on, he or she can come to stay with you for holidays or...' Her voice petered out.

Lucien pulled his gaze away as pain sliced his belly. Was that feeling of loss, the sharp stab through his gut, because he wouldn't get to raise his child? Because he'd be a long-distance parent?

Or because Aurélie was leaving?

But that was a good thing. The alternative, of her living close enough to see regularly, would be a mistake.

He tried to be a decent man. He was doing his duty by his country. Yet no bridegroom, even in an arranged marriage, should promise his life to one woman when he felt like *this* about another.

Suddenly he was on his feet, pacing the sitting room and back to the mantelpiece, staring down into the orange tongues of flame.

Aurélie's timing was terrible. He was about to escort Ilsa to an official dinner. There was no time for proper discussion. Had Aurélie known that? Had she chosen her moment deliberately?

'I'm sorry. I guess you're disappointed.' Aurélie rose and moved towards him. In well-worn jeans and a figure-hugging long-sleeved black top, she looked far too sexy. Her hair was a bright, glowing halo and her downturned pout drew his hungry gaze.

As she approached Lucien stiffened then saw her register the movement. She pulled up short. Did he imagine a bruised look of distress in her eyes?

'I know it seems mad not to accept your offer. I'm denying our child the right to inherit all this.' She waved her arm wide. 'But when it came to the crunch, I can't leave it here. It's my child. I want to know it, love it, care for it. I want it to know and love me too.'

Lucien's mouth twisted.

Did she think he didn't want that?

He'd lost his family, not once but twice. First as a baby when his parents had died in an accident and then more recently with the deaths of his aunt, uncle and cousin. At least Aurélie had family, even if they weren't close.

He had no one. He'd try to care for Ilsa. But, despite their mutual respect, he doubted there'd ever be a deep connection.

That wasn't Aurélie's fault. They were in an impossible situation. One of them had to lose. Yet that didn't stop the hollow ache of emptiness.

'It's probably just as well.' His voice emerged like gravel from his constricted throat. 'I don't know anything about babies.'

But he could learn. It surprised him how much he wanted to learn. How much, as the days passed and the baby's existence became more real, he looked forward to being part of its life.

He forced a lighter tone. 'When he's older he can visit.'

But was that any way to build a relationship? Occasional visits when the child was old enough to travel? Surely the parental bond began earlier. Didn't he owe it to his baby to be there from the beginning?

Lucien dragged his fingers through his hair, torn by conflicting emotions. The need to respect her wishes versus the need to act, to stop Aurélie from making what felt like a huge mistake.

'You might change your mind about that. Once you're married…' she paused '…visits from an illegitimate child could be an embarrassment.'

Lucien didn't pause to think. He took a single long pace that brought him right into her personal space, his hands gripping her slender arms through soft cotton sleeves.

'Don't even *think* of going there!' He dragged in a deep breath then realised his error when the scent of lilacs filtered to his brain. He recalled that delicious perfume from his night in her bed. 'If you think I'd let public opinion keep me from my child you're totally wrong. Do you understand?'

His fingers tightened on her arms and he leaned closer, needing to be sure there were no doubts about this. 'I won't have you pretending you know how I feel about this baby, or deciding I don't want to see it.' Lucien heard the grim note in his voice and sucked in a deep breath.

'I will be part of this child's life from the beginning. Get used to it, Aurélie. Don't try to fob me off or pretend to anyone ever, *especially* to our child, that I don't care.'

His jaw ached with tension and his heart thundered high against his ribs.

He didn't like what she'd decided. He wanted to force her hand. But he couldn't let her set up barriers between him and their child.

'I'd never do that.' Her eyes looked huge as she tilted her face up. 'Honestly.' Her palm pressed to her chest as if her heart beat hard like his. 'If you really want to be involved—'

'I do. How many times do I have to say it?'

Her lips flattened and her earnest gaze searched his. 'There's a difference between your legitimate, adopted heir and an illegitimate—'

'Don't!' he snarled, control slipping. 'Don't label our child that way. Especially as you're the one making it so.' He would have adopted their baby, made it legitimate. Lucien saw her eyes widen and snagged a deep breath. 'I will love this child whether it has my name or not.'

He might have been born into a family with a proud royal lineage, but a person was a person, their value not limited by lines on a paper.

The knowledge that Aurélie, and no doubt others, expected him to treat this child differently struck his pride and his budding paternal instincts.

'I'm sorry.' Her hand lifted to splay against his shirt front. Lucien felt instant warmth as if her touch imprinted a brand on his flesh. Heat sank deep within him, past flesh to bones. 'I know you care.' She paused and when she spoke again he had to bend his head to catch her words. 'My emotions are all over the place and trying to decide what to do for the best has been so tough.'

She blinked and Lucien saw her eyes glisten, over-bright. Her bottom lip trembled before she clamped it with pearly teeth.

A curious sensation rose within him. Tenderness and a compulsion to shield her.

He reached out and brushed back a curl of burnished hair that had escaped her ponytail. It was silky smooth and he found his hand anchoring in her hair instead of letting go.

'It will work out, you'll see,' he murmured, as much to himself as her. 'Between us this child will be loved and well cared for.'

She nodded and offered him a trusting smile of piercing sweetness.

Lucien's breath caught. Everything stilled as he looked deep into Aurélie's eyes. The world narrowed to nothing but her and him, this moment, and the craving he battled to contain.

His fingers tightened around satiny hair. The weight of her palm on his chest seemed heavier by the moment. He needed to step back, he knew that, but knowing and acting were separate things. Especially with the addictive scent of spring flowers and warm woman teasing his nostrils.

'Aurélie…' His voice was a murmured rumble, cut off when another sound intruded. He looked up, past her shoulder.

There, her hand on the now open door, stood his fiancée.

'Hello, Aurélie, Lucien.' Ilsa's voice broke the spell.

Aurélie stiffened, her heart jamming high in her throat. Had she been leaning up towards Lucien or had he been bending to her?

For a second longer her fingers clutched the pristine white of his formal shirt, feeling his body heat seep into hers. Then, with a gasp of horror, she stepped back.

Lucien's eyes were unreadable but her own thoughts fed her guilt.

They'd started out discussing their baby. They'd argued and somehow ended up close enough for her to feel the thud of his heart and the urgent need to be closer. She'd remembered the taste of his kiss and wished she could relive it one final time.

Until Ilsa spoke.

Aurélie licked her lips, realising her mouth was bone-dry. Lucien's gaze flickered on the movement and electricity zapped through her, puckering nipples and drawing her flesh tight.

She shuddered and they both stepped back.

She didn't hear Ilsa approach over the thrumming of blood in her ears. But when she turned, the Princess was there, gorgeous in a dress of sky-blue silk. She wore bright blue gems at her ears and throat.

As Aurélie watched, Lucien turned to his fiancée. 'Ilsa. We were discussing the baby. Aurélie has decided against us adopting.'

Ilsa's gaze caught hers and Aurélie found herself holding her breath. Because she liked the woman and guessed she'd be disappointed by the decision?

Or because of the swamping guilt? She'd been caught leaning into Lucien, silently begging for his kiss.

Heat flamed her cheeks. Surely she'd never come on to another woman's man? What had she been thinking?

Besides, look at this pair. They were perfect together.

Her gaze skated from Ilsa to Lucien, his formal eveningwear emphasising his lean, dark handsomeness and rangy athletic frame. Even the golden glow of his skin against the snowy shirt seemed to reinforce the difference between him and ordinary people like her.

Seeing them together, ready for their royal event, made a mockery of Aurélie's crazy dreams. Here she was in jeans and a T-shirt top, while they... They looked exactly what they were. Inhabitants of a rarefied world she could never be part of.

It was as well she'd decided to go. Any other option would be impossible.

Ilsa spoke. 'Aurélie, we need to—'

She didn't want to hear any more. Not while her pulse still pounded in anticipation of Lucien's mouth on hers. 'I'm sorry. I can't discuss this any more now. I'm very tired.'

She hurried to the door, filled with guilt and shame. Tomorrow, early, she'd go home.

For everyone's sake, especially her own, she couldn't stay here any longer.

CHAPTER NINE

'WHAT DO YOU MEAN, I can't leave?'

Lucien's assistant winced as Aurélie's voice hit a high note. She strove to calm herself.

She was stressed. Sleep had been impossible last night. She'd spent hours tossing and turning, burning with regret as she relived the moment she'd been caught by Lucien's fiancée, trying to kiss him. For, no matter how she evaded the truth, that was what she'd been doing. *Willing* him to lean in and take her mouth.

She shivered at the memory.

As a result, she'd fallen asleep around dawn and woken so late that the meal she'd just finished in her room was lunch rather than breakfast.

She'd hoped to be on a bus out of the country this morning.

'His Majesty wants to see you. He asked that you do him the courtesy of waiting here.' For the first time since she'd met the royal secretary he looked almost disapproving. 'If you wouldn't mind waiting, Ms Balland? The King won't be long. He's had a very busy morning.'

Naturally. He had a country to run.

As for her desire to leave immediately… What had she been thinking? She mightn't want to face him and she hoped Ilsa wouldn't be with him, but Aurélie owed him a goodbye. And thanks for his hospitality. Besides, they had to make arrangements for the baby.

'Of course.' She summoned a smile. 'There are things we need to discuss.'

She looked at her backpack by the door. 'I don't suppose you know if there are any buses leaving for France in the afternoon, do you? I haven't been able to get online to check.'

Last night she'd taken refuge in a long soak in the sunken bathtub, trying to relax. Unfortunately, she'd dropped her phone, seeing it crack on the marble then plunge into the water.

'You haven't been online?'

'No. My phone is damaged. Does that mean you don't know about buses?' She frowned as she took in his arrested expression. Maybe people in palaces didn't catch buses.

'I'm afraid I don't, but I'll find out for you.'

He withdrew from her sitting room, leaving her with her thoughts. She hadn't woken to nausea and, despite feeling miserable, had more energy than she'd had in days.

Because she'd made a decision? Because she was making a clean break, distancing herself from Lucien?

She didn't want to think about that. It might be the right thing to do, but it felt terrible. Which was ridiculous. She barely knew the man she was already missing.

With a *hmph* of self-disgust she opened her pack, took out the textbook she'd brought and settled to wait.

When she didn't respond to his knock, Lucien opened the door.

Aurélie was curled up in the corner of the sofa, eyes closed, a book open on her knees.

Lucien paused, his heart skipping as he took her in.

Given the high-octane tension gripping the palace, it seemed impossible that she slept.

Seeing her relaxed, her hair spilling across the cushions, reminded him of the morning he'd left her in bed. He'd had to force himself to leave. The temptation to stay and deny the demands of the real world had been so strong.

Now the real world intruded with a vengeance.

His mouth tightened as he thought of this morning's work. The long discussions with Ilsa and others last night and today. The press release and its instantaneous results. The road in front of the palace jammed with royal-watchers.

And here was Aurélie, oblivious. With her soft curls escaping her ponytail, wearing jeans and a shirt of vibrant purple, her socks striped in different shades of purple, she looked about eighteen.

And innocent.

His gaze dipped to her abdomen where, even in sleep, one palm rested protectively.

Back in his office, dealing with one official after

another, he'd had a moment of doubt. Most considered his actions crazy. But standing here, watching the woman who carried his unborn child, he knew with a deep certainty that he'd made the right decision.

Interestingly, both Ilsa and his secretary agreed, though the latter hadn't said so explicitly. He, like the rest of Lucien's personal staff, was too busy dealing with the ramifications of this morning's announcement.

Lucien walked to the sofa and lifted the book from Aurélie's legs before it slid to the floor. Psychology. Was that what she wanted to study?

He imagined she'd be good at it. He remembered her interest in other people at the restaurant. Her ability to read character and respond in a way that left customers smiling and, in one case, defused potential trouble.

'Lucien?' Her voice was husky with sleep, running up his spine like the brush of velvet.

He smiled at her, enjoying the warmth in her unguarded eyes and the supple twist of her slim body as she stretched. For this moment it felt again as if they shared that remarkable unspoken communion.

Till her eyebrows snapped down and she sat up, mouth flattening. 'You wanted to see me.'

It sounded like an accusation. He remembered being told she was ready to leave for the bus station. Did she really think she'd walk away from him so easily?

'Yes. We have things to discuss.' He gestured to the backpack propped by the wall. 'Is that all your luggage?'

She nodded.

'Good. We'll talk on the way.' Because after the tense night and fraught morning he'd had, Lucien was ready to get out. 'I need fresh air.'

Huge eyes met his with an expression that made his stomach drop away. 'You're driving me to the bus station?'

She ripped off the band securing her hair back and for a second she looked like an angel painted by some old master. All big eyes, glorious hair and translucent skin. Then she yanked her hair back and tied it in her usual ponytail.

Lucien wanted to tell her to leave it loose. No doubt she'd object and they had more important matters to negotiate.

'You wanted to leave the palace, didn't you?'

She nodded. Did he imagine she looked disappointed? Maybe she wasn't so eager to leave after all.

'I'll take you somewhere quiet where we can settle the details.' The palace was buzzing with excitement and speculation and he'd had enough. There'd be no real escape from public curiosity after this morning, but even half an hour's respite would be welcome.

Aurélie nodded jerkily and reached for her boots. Moments later she was on her feet. Lucien swung her pack over his shoulder, stifling her protest with a look, then shepherded her out.

They took a secret exit from the palace, driving an unmarked dark blue sports car and emerging from a tunnel known only to a few palace intimates. They emerged a block behind the official back entrance.

Just as well. Even here there were more cars than usual. According to Security, the throng of onlookers at the palace perimeter was now three deep.

Lucien sighed and concentrated on manoeuvring through the busy streets. He didn't regret what he'd done. But there were still obstacles to be overcome.

Including the obstinacy of this woman.

For fifteen minutes Aurélie was silent, then as he nosed the car towards an exit from the city, she spoke. 'Where are we going? This can't be the way to the bus stop.'

'No, we're going to my place.'

She spun round towards him. 'Your place? Don't you live in the palace?'

Lucien took another off ramp, heading not towards the highway that ringed the city, but another road that led through green farmland towards the head of the valley.

'Sometimes.' He felt the corners of his mouth tuck in. 'I've stayed there since returning to Vallort because it's convenient, given the huge amount of work to be done.' And because he hadn't wanted to face the drive to his family home, up the winding road where Justin had met his death. A deep-seated shudder racked him and he tightened his grip on the wheel.

'But I don't think of it as home.' It was magnificent, ideal for royal events, but its grandiose formality made it a showpiece not a home. 'Much of the palace is used for government administration. There's a museum in one wing and some of the larger spaces are available for public events like concerts and conferences.' He paused, slowing to take a narrow bridge. 'Usually the royal family stays there for major functions or to host international VIPs.'

'Like Princess Ilsa?'

'Exactly.'

'I should talk to her. Explain about last night.'

Lucien turned to see Aurélie frowning at a massive waterfall dropping down a cliff on the other side of the valley.

'There's no need. Ilsa and I have spoken about that.'

Aurélie turned to catch his gaze, her expression worried. 'She understood? About what she saw? I didn't mean to—'

'She understood completely.' Lucien felt again that dragging weight of shame and relief in his gut.

Ilsa had known exactly what she'd seen when she'd opened the door on them last night. It had made their later discussion much easier, though Lucien had never felt so uncomfortable in his life.

He hadn't actually kissed Aurélie and he'd told himself he'd have pulled back before it came to that. But it had been a relief not to have to pretend indifference any more. It had been tearing him apart.

Lucien had never been indifferent to Aurélie, though he'd tried for Ilsa's sake. Last night any thought of dissembling had been ripped away.

Even now, after a sleepless night and hours fraught with diplomatic difficulties, Lucien was glad.

'Nevertheless, I should talk to her.'

'She's gone.'

'Gone?'

Lucien felt Aurélie's gaze as he swung the car round a curve at the end of a tranquil lake and took a turn that headed into deep forest.

'She left for Altbourg this morning. I drove her to the airport.'

They'd parted amicably. Remarkably so, in the circumstances. But he suspected Ilsa had her own reasons for supporting him as he faced this watershed moment.

'Oh.'

Lucien's mouth twisted wryly. He'd been told Aurélie hadn't heard today's news. He suspected she'd have a lot more to say when she did.

'I'd hate to think I hurt her. I like her. She's very nice.'

'She is.'

Aurélie said no more. Which was good as Luc-

ien had other matters on his mind as he guided the car around a hairpin bend then accelerated on the upward climb. His whole being, body and mind, tensed and the skin between his shoulder blades prickled.

It was the first time he'd driven this way since his return to Vallort.

He knew this road like the back of his hand.

But then so had Justin.

Aurélie subsided into silence. She felt terrible about last night. No matter what she tried to convince herself, she *had* wanted to kiss Lucien. She'd wanted to melt into his embrace and feel his mouth on hers.

Heat scored her cheeks as she thought of Princess Ilsa and how Aurélie had wronged her, trying to seduce her fiancé.

Mouth compressing, she focused on her surroundings. How far were they travelling? She should have asked but had been too caught up in their conversation.

She tried to summon annoyance that Lucien was taking her out of the city when she had a bus to catch. But they needed to talk about future arrangements. She had no doubt he'd have someone help get her on a bus when they'd finished. Besides, she was curious to see Lucien's home.

And, the dangerous thought hovered, maybe despite her determination, she wasn't eager to say her final goodbyes.

Aurélie watched the rock wall of a cutting slide by as the low-slung car purred around another bend then surged forward on the straight. The view was spectacular. She looked out of the far window to a perfect vista of green valley dotted with traditional wooden farm buildings and beyond that the foothills of snow-capped mountains. But what caught her eye was Lucien's profile. His expression was grim, his brow furrowed and jaw locked.

'Is everything all right?' she asked as they rounded another curve and a couple of workmen came into view. A truck was parked in a layby and they seemed to be inspecting a retaining wall.

Lucien expelled his breath in a sigh. He slowed the car and lowered the window. One of the men raised an arm in greeting. Lucien responded, calling out something in a language she didn't know. The workers nodded. Then the car inched forward.

Aurélie saw an ugly bare patch above the new retaining wall, barren of vegetation. Turning, she noticed a break in the treetops below them on the other side of the road.

'Has there been an avalanche?'

'It's okay.' Lucien's voice held an unfamiliar rough note. 'The whole mountainside has been surveyed and the necessary work completed.'

Aurélie nodded. 'That's good. You wouldn't want to have an...' Her words stopped as she recalled the press report about his cousin. A rockfall after

storms and heavy rain on the road from his residence.

She gasped as the implication sank in.

Lucien's hands tightened on the wheel. 'It's safe now. I wouldn't risk you or the baby.' Still that deep voice didn't sound like his. Her heart squeezed as she recognised pain.

'Are you all right, driving here?'

Briefly his eyes met hers and she felt a jangle of sensation in her midriff.

'You know about Justin?'

Aurélie nodded. 'I read about the accident.'

Lucien turned back to the road, manoeuvring the powerful car with ease. 'It should never have happened. They knew that area needed attention. There'd been a small slip the month before. But I'm told he was distracted by my uncle's failing health, even when warned of the danger, and didn't order the necessary work.' Aurélie heard strain in his tone and read tension in his powerful frame. 'I'm having every mountain road in Vallort surveyed and upgraded where necessary.'

Aurélie's heart wrung at the ache in his thickened voice. She reached out and lightly touched his upper arm. 'I'm so sorry, Lucien. I know he meant a lot to you.'

She remembered his terrible blankness the night they'd met, as if, trapped in the depths of grief, the world no longer made sense.

'Thank you.' Then, before she had time to say

more, they rounded another curve and pulled up in a wide levelled space with the valley on one side, the mountain on the other and dead ahead the most wondrous building she'd ever seen.

It looked like a castle from a storybook. She half expected to see some medieval princess or a knight in armour emerge from the entrance. Or a fairy godmother.

'You *live* here?'

From this angle the castle looked taller than it was wide. It was built of pale stone and sprouted a forest of towers with conical roofs. Curiously, the tops of some towers were whitewashed and half-timbered, softening the effect of grim stone. Afternoon sun shone on mullioned windows and on roof tiles of a deep, rich green that, in this moment of whimsy, made Aurélie think of dragon scales. From the tallest tower flew the royal green and white banner of Vallort.

She'd left the real world and entered a fairy story.

'This is where I grew up.'

Aurélie shook her head. 'I can't imagine it.' It was a far cry from the cramped rented home where she'd been raised. 'You live here?'

She turned to see Lucien's face grow mask-like. 'I will now. It was time to leave the city.'

That was right. He'd said he hadn't been living here. Aurélie surveyed his taut features and thought of that ugly slashing scar on the mountainside below. Was that why? Had there been too many memories here?

It was none of her business but she felt tenderness well up. Without stopping to think she touched his arm, feeling the rigid strength of his biceps.

'Welcome home.'

He jerked his head around from contemplating the castle. Those remarkable eyes flared brighter as they captured hers and something tugged deep within. Not just the sexual tension that always simmered around this man, but something more profound. Her hand settled on his arm, fingers gently squeezing.

'Thank you, Aurélie.' He covered her hand with his.

Again it wasn't a sexually charged gesture, though the warmth of his touch sent heat shimmering through her. This was about comfort given and acknowledged and it felt utterly natural.

Aurélie refused to consider whether she had the right to comfort him. Soon she'd be leaving. Time enough for regrets then. She sucked in a quick breath at the sudden ache filling her chest.

Lucien turned back towards the castle. 'It was a good place to grow up. There are lots of happy memories.' His lips curved. 'Justin and I had a ball, playing here. It's a paradise for kids.'

Aurélie flinched and pulled her hand away.

She guessed he hadn't said it deliberately but Lucien's words reminded her that she was depriving her child of so much, choosing to raise it alone, rather than here as part of the royal family.

'You wanted to talk.' Her voice sounded flat. Which she supposed was better than revealing the tumult of her conflicting emotions.

'Yes, come inside.'

The building was everything she'd expected from the outer view, and more. Its ancient origins were clear to see but blended with modern comfort.

Built around a large central courtyard, the place was actually circular. They entered through a vaulted hall that looked as if it could host a banquet for a couple of hundred. The massive fireplaces were so big she could have stood up in them. Huge, beautiful tapestries lined the walls and above them was an incredible display of old weapons.

They were greeted by an older couple who Lucien explained ran the castle, with help. But they were more than staff, Aurélie decided when she saw the housekeeper blink back tears as she welcomed Lucien and heard the warmth in their voices as they exchanged greetings.

'What was that you were speaking?' she asked as she and Lucien made their way up a broad, handsomely carved staircase.

'The ancient language of the mountains. It's one of our national languages, along with French and German. It's spoken mainly in the country areas though there's a bit of a revival in the city. This way.' He opened a panelled door and stood back.

Aurélie walked in then stopped, eyes widening and jaw dropping. After a couple of moments she stepped forward, drawn by the vista.

'This is incredible,' she whispered. The ceiling was high and the whole wall before her, from knee level up, was a vast expanse of glass facing out over the valley to the mountains on the other side. It was so beautiful it stole her breath.

She reached the window and experienced a moment's vertigo. Below her was a sheer drop into a chasm where white water sprayed and swirled on its way down to a waterfall. Sunlight caught droplets of moisture on the air, creating a miniature rainbow that reinforced her earlier sense that this was a fantastic, magical place.

'You like it?'

'I haven't got the words. It's amazing.' She turned to see Lucien beside her, a smile turning his face from solemn to irresistibly attractive.

She sucked in a fortifying breath and made herself turn back to the view. 'I thought it would be dark and gloomy inside.'

'Some parts are, since it was originally built for defence. Fortunately, some of my predecessors decided to renovate. Most of the rooms away from the front have large windows. We also have decent heating and a couple of lifts so you don't have to climb endless staircases unless you want to.'

Dragging her attention from the view, she surveyed the big sitting room with its plump upholstered sofas, gleaming wood and beautiful carpets that looked like ones she'd seen in museums. There was an enormous bookcase on one wall, filled with paperbacks as well as more serious-looking tomes, and bowls of spring flowers on small tables. The effect was of restrained luxury but, above all, comfort.

Something inside her eased. She didn't feel intimidated here as she had in the gilded palace. This was a home, not a showpiece. Even if it was inside the most fabulous fairy tale castle.

Her gaze settled on the polished dark wood of a grand piano, sporting an array of photos in silver frames. Aurélie wanted to investigate, guessing they were family portraits. Would there be photos of Lucien as a child? Of his family?

But she wasn't here to explore. He wanted to discuss arrangements for their baby.

'Please take a seat,' he said as the housekeeper entered with a tray.

Settling into the corner of a cosy sofa, Aurélie was relieved to discover the tray held a pot of tea along with home-made biscuits and cake, but no coffee. Had Lucien warned his staff?

He waited till they were both seated and she'd had a sip of tea before speaking. 'We've got important things to decide, Aurélie.'

'I know.' It had been stupid to think of leaving without seeing him. But she'd been spooked by the strength of her reaction to him, how close she'd come last night to doing something regrettable. Even now, her body hummed with tension, with need. 'We have to agree to some arrangements.'

'Especially as circumstances have changed.'

'They have?' Reading his serious expression, Aurélie guessed it wasn't good news. She stiffened, her mind racing. 'Is something wrong? Did my blood test show a problem with the baby?' She put down her tea and braced her hands on the edge of her seat, heart pounding.

'No, nothing like that. As far as I know, the baby is fine.'

Aurélie sank back, catching her breath. The baby was fine. That was all that mattered.

The moment of intense fear simplified everything, revealing the bond she already felt with her child. She *was* doing the right thing, choosing to raise it.

'What *has* changed is my status.'

'You're not King any more?' She frowned and his mouth curved in a wry smile that tugged a cord deep inside her.

Desperation beat at her. Aurélie could no longer deny her weakness for this man. She barely knew him yet it felt as if she knew everything she needed to, and liked it all.

She needed to leave *soon*. Her fingers tightened on the seat beneath her. Being near him was pure torment.

'It would take a lot for that to change. Apart

from anything else, I'm the last of my line.' He paused, his smile fading, and Aurélie wondered if his thoughts had strayed to his dead cousin. She recalled Lucien's expression as they'd passed the scene of the rockfall. He was still grieving.

'No, what's changed is that I'm no longer engaged. Ilsa and I agreed last night to end our betrothal.'

Aurélie opened her mouth then closed it again. Finally she spoke, her dry mouth making her voice husky. 'Because of me? Because of what happened last night?'

'That was the catalyst. But the truth is, neither of us was eager to marry.'

Aurélie felt about an inch tall. Her cheeks burned. Yet at the same time she felt like rejoicing.

'I'm so sorry. I—'

'There's no need to apologise. Ilsa and I were relieved to end it.'

Aurélie stared, wondering if that were true. Did he really believe that? He and the Princess were so well-matched. Besides that, she'd never met a man more magnetically attractive than Lucien. He had charisma as well as good looks, a depth of character that appealed as much as his charm. Had Ilsa *really* wanted to end the engagement or had she felt forced to?

'But it was all arranged! Everyone was preparing for the wedding.'

He inclined his head. As he did the light from the

windows shifted, or maybe she just saw him more clearly, registering the signs of weariness around his eyes and mouth.

'Yes. It's taking some organising.'

'But the Princess's family! Won't they be upset?' Surely breaking off the betrothal at this late date would cause offence? Plus the two countries were on the verge of new financial and economic arrangements. Wasn't this the worst possible timing?

'There are some issues.' Lucien's voice, as much as his expression, confirmed her thoughts. 'But our decision was mutual. Ilsa and I agreed the marriage wouldn't be in our best interests and, as a result, not in our countries' interests.'

He wrapped his hand around the back of his neck as if to ease some stiffness there. Aurélie wondered if it was due to stress. 'There's some diplomatic fallout and a whole lot of media interest, but we'll get through it.'

'I'm so sorry.' She wanted to reach out to him but forced herself to sit still. 'I feel responsible.'

Lucien shrugged. 'Let's face it. Whatever arrangement we made about our baby was bound to be problematic, with me married to Ilsa. At least this simplifies things.'

Aurélie was busy telling herself there was nothing momentous about the way Lucien said *our baby*, yet she couldn't deny her shiver of delight at his words.

'I suppose it does.' Two parents instead of three

made decision-making easier. And though she liked Ilsa, Aurélie wasn't keen on her child having a step-mother.

Though that would come one day, when Lucien chose another royal bride.

'Of course it does.' Lucien leaned forward, his eyes snaring hers. 'Now I'm free I can do what I should have from the start. Marry me, Aurélie, and we'll bring up our baby together.'

CHAPTER TEN

'YOU CAN'T BE SERIOUS!'

Lucien stared into Aurélie's dazed eyes and reminded himself to be patient. She hadn't been expecting this. Yet he'd expected more enthusiasm.

Disappointment stirred. He'd seen the desire in her eyes last night. He'd read her body language. She'd wanted him then, as she'd wanted him before. That couldn't have changed in one night.

But was attraction, even the profound desire they shared, enough? Royal life was a privilege but a burden too. Would the prospect of it scare her into saying no?

Lucien couldn't accept that. Not if he was to look after Aurélie and their baby as they deserved.

'Never more serious. Now there's nothing stopping us from taking the obvious step that's best for our child. Marry and raise it together.'

Aurélie's mouth opened and closed but no sound emerged. Her eyes grew enormous.

'But we… We're not…' She shook her head and slumped back in her seat.

Anyone would think he'd given her bad news instead of inviting her to marry him. Disquiet niggled his belly.

She looked at him as if he'd grown a second head. As if his proposal were preposterous. As if she denied what was between them.

Lucien thought of the women who'd insinuated themselves into his life, or downright pushed their way in, and that was while he had no expectation of inheriting a throne. The number who'd been eager to try persuading him into a long-term relationship.

Was this some sort of cosmic justice that the only woman he'd ever proposed to didn't want him?

The knowledge grated, harsh and raw, shredding his pride and bringing something close to hurt.

With Ilsa he'd inherited a fiancée. There'd been no proposal, no choice. This time he'd acted of his own volition, trying to do what was right by the baby, and by Aurélie, yet she looked as if he'd insulted her.

Lucien's jaw clenched and his body stiffened.

Nothing in his experience with the opposite sex had prepared him for rejection.

He watched her shoot to her feet, step away then stop. As if she didn't know what to do with herself.

Lucien knew the feeling. He was a jumble of emotions he preferred not to analyse. He forced a calm voice as he got up to stand before her.

'We *are* an item, Aurélie. There's a bond between us nothing can erase. We're lovers, and we're having a baby.'

'Ex-lovers.' The word shot out.

Her instantaneous repudiation felt like a physical blow.

All this time he'd struggled to do his duty by his country and his family's memory, and by Ilsa.

He'd fought but been unable to banish his response to Aurélie.

He'd been through hell in the past day, bearing the brunt of Altbourg's disapproval at the broken engagement, the threat of severed diplomatic and economic ties, and the outrage of his own councillors. Thankfully the worst was over and, with Ilsa's help, relations with her country would be smoothed out.

Lucien had stood firm because finally he had the chance to do the *right* thing. He knew in his bones that marrying Aurélie and raising their child together was his future.

'It's not over between us, Aurélie. You know it.' He moved closer, invading her space. He drew in her distinctive lilac scent and felt something unfurl inside him.

Yet the stubborn woman shook her head, her mouth a mutinous line. 'It's over, Lucien. That was two months ago.'

'Two months and four days.'

He'd tried not to count them. He'd had plenty to fill his time, taking a crown and a fiancée. Maybe that was part of why he hadn't been able to erase Aurélie from his thoughts. Remembering their night together had been a bright flame during the long, burdened days and nights.

She looked shocked that he knew the number of days. Even so her chin rose. 'It's finished and—'

'Liar.' He closed his hands around her upper arms.

Instead of wrenching free or demanding that he released her, after one swift inhale Aurélie's muscles loosened. Lucien saw her bottom lip tremble and remembered the taste of her, rich and seductive.

Triumph burst through him in a rush of molten heat.

'It's not finished, is it, Aurélie?'

Oh, no. Not anywhere near it.

This time, the bond between them didn't feel like weakness. Its potency resonated through him.

The long wait was over.

Lucien slid an arm around Aurélie's waist and pulled her in. Heat to heat. Body to body. So close he saw the jittering pulse at her throat and felt her exhalation against his throat.

He waited, unmoving.

Giving her time to pull back?

Not likely! He felt a tremor rip through her and knew it for excitement. The same excitement he felt, holding her again.

No, he gave her time to admit she felt it too, the magnetic pull between them.

Still she avoided his eyes. 'We shouldn't. We can't…'

Lucien had spent the last two months hemmed in by restrictions and expectations. By everything he was supposed to do and not supposed to do, including who he was expected to marry. He'd had enough. Last night he'd ripped free, creating an international incident in the process. He had no intention of letting Aurélie play coy now.

'We *can* and we definitely *will*. That's a promise.'

He turned her head up, forcing her to meet his gaze. She didn't try to pull away. Instead her pupils dilated and her lips parted and Lucien felt his soul sing as he tilted his head down and took her mouth.

Yes. This.

One touch of lips on lips and it was like flame to tinder-dry kindling. Lucien almost heard the whoosh of ignition as restraint exploded and their mouths clung.

He moved, angling his head for better access, and found her already shifting to accommodate him.

His arm tightened around her waist, hauling her up against him. His other hand was in her hair, re-learning the silky texture, tugging free the band that held it back, so a froth of soft waves tickled him.

Lucien's eyes shut, the better to concentrate on searing delight.

Aurélie's hands went to his shoulders, clinging as if to ensure he didn't let her go. She had nothing to worry about. He had no intention of stopping.

Lucien kissed her deeply, lapping up the taste of her, exulting in the ravenous demands of her tongue tangling with his. Swallowing the little humming sounds of appreciation and encouragement she made.

She was so enthusiastic, so attuned to him, he was already hard.

So much for her pretence she didn't want him. She pressed her lithe body up against his as if nothing mattered but the need to touch and be touched.

His arm dropped from her waist so he could cup her buttocks and pull her closer.

It was as if he'd flicked a switch. Aurélie bucked her hips against him and Lucien saw stars as all the blood rushed to his groin. She ground her lower body against him, emitting a sound somewhere between a groan and a purr. That felt so good. So incredibly good he needed more. Now!

Breathing ragged, hands soldered to her eager body, he opened his eyes enough to scan the room.

Right behind her was a sofa. Long enough to take his tall frame and roomy enough for the pair of them.

But Lucien wanted more than a quick tumble before someone bustled in to collect the tray. He wanted Aurélie, all of her, and he wanted privacy.

Still with his mouth locked on Aurélie's, he bent, sliding his arms around her, and hoisted her up against his chest.

'What are you—?'

'What do you think? I'm taking you to bed.'

She didn't utter a word of protest. Instead her eyes took on a glow that matched the fire in his belly.

At last she'd given up on denial. The clutch of

her fingers around the back of his neck betrayed urgency. Her breasts rose and fell quickly as if she couldn't suck in enough oxygen. He knew the feeling. His lungs laboured, not from effort but anticipation.

He was heading for the staircase to his private suite when he heard a sound behind him. A sharp rap on the outer door and the sound of someone clearing their throat.

Silently Lucien cursed. Every muscle stiffened and his jaw gritted. How often in childhood had he heard that sound? Inevitably it had been Henri, the family's ultra-discreet major-domo, come to inform the King of some urgent interruption that would drag Uncle Joseph, groaning, away from his family and back to work.

Lucien knew he could trust implicitly in Henri's discretion. He also knew that he'd never interrupt unless it was vital. He was incredibly protective of the royal family's privacy. In some ways he was like a family member.

Lucien had hoped to carve out a few hours of privacy with Aurélie, but he'd been kidding himself. Today he'd dropped a grenade into the well-oiled machinery of government and international diplomacy and the consequences had been cataclysmic.

Soon, though. Soon he'd have Aurélie to himself. He vowed it.

The knock came again.

With a superhuman effort he turned and lowered

Aurélie so she stood beside him. He wrapped his arm around her, holding her close when she wobbled. He pressed his lips to her hair, whispering words of reassurance.

'Yes, Henri?' he called.

The door opened and Henri appeared, his gaze fixed on the tea tray at the end of the sofa rather than the room's occupants.

'I'm sorry to interrupt, Your Majesty. It's the Prime Minister. He says he needs to meet you again urgently. He's offered to drive up to the castle—'

'No!' That was something Lucien had learned from his uncle. To keep official meetings away from home. To preserve some sort of private life.

Lucien looked down at Aurélie's bright hair and felt again that clench of hungry possessiveness. And some emotion he guessed stemmed from the fact she carried his baby.

If they were going to have a private family life, he needed to safeguard it, beginning now. Of course he'd spend hours of his so-called private time doing official paperwork, but he wouldn't turn their home into a meeting place for government officials.

It struck Lucien that the castle *was* home, no matter how reluctant he'd been to return.

The first time driving past the spot where Justin died had been tough, but here, in the place where he'd spent so many happy years, he felt only comfort.

And anticipation. He squeezed Aurélie's waist

and her eyes met his. Immediately heat reignited in his belly, and he silently cursed the Prime Minister, even though he was doing his job.

'Ask my secretary to set up a meeting in the palace—' he glanced at his watch '—in an hour.'

'Very good, Your Majesty.'

What had just happened?

With dazed eyes Aurélie looked from the withdrawing butler to Lucien's serious expression.

Inevitably her gaze slid to his mouth, to those lips that had taken her to the edge of paradise.

What a kiss!

She'd been putty in his hands, not just acquiescent but collaborating in her own seduction.

Because Lucien had insisted it wasn't over between them.

Because he knew to the day how long they'd been apart. Her stupid heart had dipped and shivered when she heard that. It had seemed impossibly romantic.

He had the power to undo her defences with a look, aside from the caress of his lips and that hungry, confident way he'd hauled her to him as if she was his.

But none of that meant she belonged here! She didn't. She never would, no matter what her wayward body felt.

She stepped back, only to discover his arm still around her waist.

'Where are you going?' he murmured and Aurélie hated herself for loving the deep gravel note of his voice, as if his body hadn't yet accepted the news that sex wasn't on the agenda.

'I can't stay here.' She didn't try to break his hold, knowing it was futile. Instead she jerked her chin higher and met his stare with what she hoped was cool confidence. 'I don't belong.'

'I want you here, which means you belong. No one else has a say in that.'

'Not even me?' Aurélie wished she could shake free of the fog engulfing her. It was hard to think because Lucien had kissed her and said he wanted her.

But then he kissed like a fallen angel, with all the skills of a born sensualist and the ruthless determination of a man used to getting his own way.

'You're being deliberately obtuse. Of course you have a say. That's why you're here, so we can talk. Among other things.'

One look from under heavy eyelids, one suggestive comment and her body fired with longing. Flames licked through her veins, flaring in deep-seated places that made her shift and look away.

Aurélie moved back, out of his hold. 'Now who's being obtuse? You're a king. You meet with the Prime Minister! I'm a waitress. I'll never belong here.'

'You have something against royalty?'

'It's not that.' He was deliberately misunderstanding. 'You can't be serious about us…marrying.' There. She'd said it. 'It's preposterous.'

His dark eyebrows furrowed into a deep V. 'You don't believe in equality? You think you're less than me because of who our parents were?'

'It's not about being less or more. It's about being…' she searched for the right word '…incompatible. I don't belong in this rarefied world.'

Blazing amber eyes held hers. 'I never thought you such a snob, Aurélie. Next you'll be saying our child doesn't belong here.'

'That's different—'

'Of course it's not. It's all about what we want and what we believe. And what we choose to teach our child.' He paused. 'As for being incompatible, we've just proved that's a lie.'

Aurélie closed her eyes, summoning patience. 'I don't mean I think you're a better person than me. I mean I don't have the background, the knowledge, to live as a princess.'

'Queen, not a princess,' he murmured and she could have clouted him.

'You're not taking this seriously!'

'Oh, believe me, Aurélie. I've never been more so.'

That rocked her back on her heels, especially when she read the expression in those glittering eyes. He might taunt and tease, but he was in earnest.

'Can't you see that our marrying would be a recipe for disaster? Your people expect you to marry royalty. Someone who can hold their own with diplomats and politicians and royals.'

'Have the two royals you've met been so terribly daunting?'

'Of course not.' He was trying to distract her. 'But I don't know anything about royal etiquette. I've never worn a full-length dress, much less a tiara, or exchanged chitchat with VIPs.'

Lucien tilted his head as if trying to see into her head. 'That's what worries you? Talking to VIPs and wearing fancy clothes?'

Aurélie folded her arms in frustration. 'Those are examples. You can't deny we come from different worlds. It would be…ridiculous.'

'On the contrary, we come from the same world.' He stepped closer, stealing all the oxygen in the room and making her gasp. 'As a couple we're anything but ridiculous. Exciting, yes. Amazing. Sublime even.'

She huffed out an impatient breath. 'You're talking about sex. Not a relationship.'

'I'm talking about both.' He paused and shrugged. 'Okay, so I'm guessing about the relationship because we haven't had much of a chance at one. But I know when I'm with you I feel grounded, not in a heavy way, but as if everything is in the right place for once.'

Aurélie stared. Lucien was the ruler of a country. He had wealth, charm and an obstinate willpower that threatened to bulldoze her into a ridiculous situation. Yet all she could think of was how happy she was to hear he felt the same.

Unless they were empty words.

'You can imagine me at a royal soirée, chatting with the great and the good?'

'I can imagine it very well. Though I have to disappoint you by observing that just because someone's a VIP, it doesn't make them good.' He smiled and went on before she could interrupt. 'You'd be the belle of the ball. Everyone would want to talk with you and I'd have my hands full fending off the men.'

Aurélie's breath hitched. It was crazy but the picture he painted, of Lucien guarding her possessively from male interest, was too appealing.

'You've got the people skills to make a fine diplomatic hostess. Not to mention your language abilities.'

She gawped at him. 'How would you know what abilities I've got?'

A smile curved his lips, making him look far too attractive. 'I sat for hours in that restaurant. You did a lot more than serve food. You negotiated and advised. You averted some nasty scenes with that tourist when he came on too strong. Somehow you let him down firmly but gently enough that he was still happy. You were kind to the young woman eating alone who looked miserable, and you dealt with both rowdy groups celebrating and families with difficult kids as if nothing fazed you.'

Aurélie stared. She knew he'd watched her, as she'd watched him, drawn by a force stronger than anything she'd known. Yet she'd never imagined him observing quite so clearly.

'You make it sound like I did something important.' She shook her head. 'It's just my job.'

He laughed. 'You have no idea, have you? I wish half our diplomats had your people skills. And what about your languages? I counted four that night.'

Aurélie took a half step back. It felt as if she was being assessed for a job.

That was exactly what he *was* doing! For if she married him she'd take on the job of being royal, which was terrifying. Yet, at the same time, having Lucien break it down into a matter of learnable skills made it seem slightly less daunting. Slightly more…possible.

'What languages do you speak?'

'Other than French? I'm fluent in German and English.' She'd loved learning them at school, for the insight it gave her into other places and people. When she'd started waitressing they were useful during the tourist season. 'I have basic Spanish and a few words of Russian.'

He nodded, as if approving. 'You're better than me. I could never get my head around Russian.'

'There's more to being royal than talking with people.'

'Actually, it's a large part of the job. So is listening. I remember you being a good listener that night we spent together, even if you don't want to listen to me now.'

'What's the point? It would never work.'

'On the contrary.' His jaw firmed and that trace of lazy amusement disappeared. 'We'll make it work. For our baby's sake. You want the best possible future for our child, don't you? We can give it a stable home, a loving family and a bright future. What more could it need?'

He was right.

The knowledge slammed into her, cutting off her protests. Everything he said was true. She was still adjusting to the idea of a baby, yet Aurélie knew what she wanted for it: love, security and a bright future.

There was just one problem. It might be the best for her child, but what about her?

She'd be the odd one out, accepted only because of her baby. She'd never fit in.

But you're used to not belonging, aren't you?

The memory of how disposable she'd been to her own family scoured deep, like sharp fingernails drawing blood.

She couldn't expect to find love in such a marriage. Lucien only considered it for the sake of the baby.

Her mouth turned down and she wrapped her

arms around herself, holding in the sadness welling up in her.

'I won't be railroaded.'

Lucien watched her with narrowed eyes. Aurélie had the feeling he read her fears and doubts. She prayed he had no idea how vulnerable she was to his arguments.

Of course he knows! You were about to have sex with him.

'Did I mention you could still do your psychology degree here in Vallort?'

Aurélie's eyes widened. 'There'd be no time. Not with royal duties and a baby.' Yet her heart beat faster at the idea.

'We'll carve out time since it's important to you.'

Lucien made it sound so simple. Maybe, with his help, it could be, lots of work and challenging, but achievable.

Did he realise how he tempted her?

'I need time to think.'

'Of course. Your luggage has been brought in. You'll stay as my guest till we agree.'

His tone made her shiver despite the room's warmth. It was the way he said *agree*, like a veiled threat, as if her one option was to change her mind and accept.

Aurélie told herself Lucien wasn't a bully. But there was something in his stance, and the implacable glitter of his eyes, that made him look not like a modern man but a warrior of old. The sort who might have defended this castle wearing a suit of armour and wielding one of those long battle swords she'd seen downstairs.

'And if I prefer to stay in the city?'

He was already shaking his head.

'You're saying I have no choice? What if I leave?'

'You'd find that difficult. Taxis can't come up here without permission and the estate boundary is patrolled.'

'I'm not your prisoner!'

'No, you're my guest.' He paused and Aurélie felt her pulse beat high in her throat as she saw again that bright, hard gleam in his eyes. Proprietorial, that was how it looked. As if she belonged to him.

She wanted to rail at him, tell him he had no right to keep her here.

Yet part of her revelled in that fierce possessiveness. Because it matched her feelings for him.

That was the secret that above all she had to hide.

'Now, if you'll excuse me, I must go.' He raised her hand to his lips, his open-mouthed kiss sending a rush of longing through her, weakening her knees and making her heart pound. Then he was gone, leaving her prey to turbulent emotion.

CHAPTER ELEVEN

AURÉLIE DIDN'T SEE Lucien again that day or the next. He sent his apologies, saying affairs of state kept him busy but he'd see her soon. Leaving her frustrated.

Yet, having watched the news, Aurélie understood he wasn't avoiding her. The broken royal engagement had rocked the country and, it seemed, the whole of Europe. Speculation was rife on the cause of the split but Lucien and Princess Ilsa refused to make a public statement.

No wonder the Prime Minister had been desperate to see Lucien. There was talk of a rift between the two nations and plans for a joint economic zone disintegrating. Aurélie felt sick, knowing she was at the heart of it all.

She told herself that was why she couldn't settle to sleep on her second night in the castle. Despite her long walk through the woods, and the delicious dinner, and even a mug of hot chocolate before bed.

Finally she gave up trying to sleep and in desperation dragged on yoga pants and a T-shirt. Stretches and gentle yoga might help relieve her tension.

It was almost midnight when she heard footsteps outside her room. Surely even Lucien's motherly housekeeper wouldn't be on duty now. She'd discreetly fussed over Aurélie since she'd discovered her retching in the bathroom this morning. Aurélie had been embarrassed, but the woman's practical kindness and encouraging smiles had finally put her at ease. So much so that Aurélie feared she'd miss being looked after when she left.

A soft knock sounded.

'Come in.'

The door opened and her breath stopped as Lucien stepped in.

From her position on the floor he looked bigger and more imposing than ever. At her eye level tailored trousers outlined rock-hard thighs. He'd taken off his jacket and tie, wearing a pale shirt with the sleeves rolled up to reveal strong forearms dusted with dark hair.

Her pulse beat hard, so hard it was a wonder he didn't hear it.

'Lucien.' Was that her voice, wispy and breathless?

'Aurélie. I expected you to be asleep.'

'You came to check?' She rose as he approached.

He stopped, fingers flexing at his sides, and she recalled the last time he'd touched her. How it had felt, wrapped in his embrace.

Eventually she remembered to breathe and his gaze lowered, tracing the T-shirt that clung to her suddenly heaving breasts. Slowly his attention moved lower. Her thin yoga pants seemed somehow negligible, as if that scorching gaze saw right through them.

Aurélie felt the crackle of heat igniting deep inside. She pushed her shoulders back, telling herself she needed to look in control. Or was she recklessly responding to the interest darkening his eyes?

'My room is at the top of the tower, above this. I saw the light under your door.'

Crazy that the thought of him sleeping just above her should feel intimate. Crazier still to feel arousal like a jag of lightning sear through her.

They weren't even in touching distance, yet the fine hairs on her arms rose as her skin prickled in awareness. Her mouth dried and she swallowed hard. In the stillness of night it felt as if no one else existed. Just them.

Aurélie tried to claw her way back to sanity. 'Have you been working all this time? You look tired.' She forced herself to focus on the signs of weariness on his handsome face. Concern knotted her stomach. 'You can't keep working such long hours.'

If he's been working all this time. Maybe he was out with someone who doesn't argue all the time.

She winced, ashamed at the thought, knowing it stemmed from her own experience, rather than anything to do with Lucien. For she suspected her father hadn't been faithful to her mother during her last illness.

Lucien wasn't like her father. In fact he couldn't be more different. She admired his honesty and sense of duty. He had more self-respect, more decency than to dally with another woman while he waited for her answer.

Lucien's mouth quirked up in a constrained smile that made her even more aware of the tension zinging between them. 'Worried about me, Aurélie? Careful, you sound almost like a wife.'

For some reason the jibe didn't hurt. What did was seeing the shadows beneath his eyes and the tight lines bracketing his mouth.

They might disagree on the future, but Lucien was doing his best by the baby and, she admitted, by her. He was dealing with nuclear-grade fallout as a result. She was worried about her future and her baby's. He had a nation to consider on top of that.

'I'm serious, Lucien.' She took a step towards him then halted. Any closer and she'd be tempted to touch, despite what her conscience said.

His shoulders lifted and seemed to spread wider, making her aware of the primal male strength behind that casual movement. 'It's been a busy couple of days. Things will get easier now.'

'Now? What's happened?'

For a second he hesitated, leaving Aurélie to wonder if he'd rather not share the details.

'The King of Altbourg has weighed in. At first he was shocked and disinclined to honour the diplomatic and economic arrangements we'd agreed on. Until Ilsa and I had a frank discussion with him.'

Aurélie felt her eyes widen. How frank had that

discussion been? Did it include mentioning her pregnancy?

'Fortunately he loves his daughter. Once he knew she genuinely wanted out of a relationship that couldn't go anywhere, he became extremely understanding.' Another shrug. 'He and his government want this new economic zone as much as we do.'

'So it's over? Everything's okay?'

Aurélie felt the weight of guilt slide from her. She hadn't done anything wrong, but she'd blamed herself.

'As far as our governments are concerned, yes.'

'You're remarkable.' At his raised eyebrows she continued. 'I didn't think you'd be able to negotiate a settlement. You talk about your inexperience as King but it seems to me Vallort is lucky to have you.'

His mouth twisted ruefully. 'It's not quite so simple. The press fallout will continue. But I don't live my life to accommodate the media.'

Aurélie had fretted about that. She'd seen how the media hounded royalty. If she stayed here, or even if she didn't, the press would be part of her life, and her child's.

'Aurélie? What is it?'

She was shocked at how easily he read her disquiet.

'I'm thinking about the stories they'll write when they find out about us.'

Lucien's gaze dropped and she realised her hand lay against her still-flat abdomen.

'If you marry me I can protect you.'

Aurélie huffed out a laugh. 'Hasn't it occurred to you that saddling yourself with me could be the worst thing from a PR point of view?'

Lucien moved closer, so close she had to lift her chin to meet his stare. 'Absolutely not.'

Then he did something that shocked her into silence. He fitted his big hand over hers where it lay against her belly. He splayed his fingers and his hot touch branded her. Like a pledge of allegiance and protection.

Or was that crazy, wishful thinking?

'Whatever anyone says, Aurélie, we've created a miracle. I intend to stand by you and our child for the rest of our lives.'

The words reverberated in the silent room, echoing not just in her ears but in the desolate places inside that had felt empty since her mother died. In all the intervening years no one had cared enough to take time and really notice her the way Lucien did, much less put her first.

It was powerful, wonderful and utterly overwhelming. Unexpected heat pricked her eyes.

'Aurélie?' Concern puckered his forehead. 'Are you okay? What have I said?'

Her smile felt ridiculously tremulous but she didn't care as she turned her hand, capturing his heat and solidity as she threaded her fingers with his.

'Something wonderful. What you said...' She shook her head. 'It sounds pathetic but I'm not used to anyone caring.'

Their eyes locked and Aurélie felt a great swoop and rise of emotion. It was so strong it caught her at the knees, making her legs tremble. Convulsively she clutched Lucien's hand.

'I care, Aurélie. Never doubt it.' His whispered words trailed like a silken caress, wrapping around her fast-beating heart.

It should have been impossible to feel so much for this man. Logic said there'd been no time to form a strong bond, or to know him properly.

Instinct, bone-deep and unwavering, disagreed.

In this moment she realised that wherever she went in the future, whatever she did, there'd always be this attachment. Even though his prime concern was their unborn child, not her.

There was more, she discovered anew as his thumb brushed hers and a ripple of sexual awareness coursed through her.

Did he feel it too?

Suddenly Lucien's concerned stare turned into something different. Beneath those dark eyebrows his amber eyes lit like flame. She felt the heat of that look down in her core and higher, where her breasts drew tight.

'I haven't stopped wanting you since that night.'

His words cut through the charged atmosphere, making her suck in a sharp breath.

She shook her head. 'You were engaged to Ilsa, remember?'

'Oh, I remember.' If anything that fiery gaze grew hotter and Aurélie felt the blood rise under her skin, scorching her breasts, throat and cheeks. 'There was never anything between Ilsa and me except a formal agreement. I admire and like the woman but I never *wanted* her. We never...' He shot Aurélie a searing look from under lowered brows. 'We didn't even kiss. Neither of us was in a hurry to marry. That was just the schedule arranged when she was supposed to marry my cousin.'

Aurélie wondered what it would be like, expected to wed and produce heirs to order. She'd imagined such dynastic arrangements had died out years before.

'But the Princess is beautiful. You must have desired her.' As soon as the words escaped she cringed inwardly. Did she sound as needy as she felt, seeking further affirmation?

'You'd think so, wouldn't you?'

He pulled back the hand that covered hers and Aurélie felt a piercing moment of regret. She'd shattered their precious closeness with her tactless questions.

Lucien drew himself up to his full, imposing height. 'In the last six months I've been so busy with work, first as an architect and now here as King, that I haven't been with any woman except you.' He paused as if letting her absorb his words.

'In that time the *only* woman I've imagined in my bed is you, Aurélie. No one else.'

Her breath hissed on a stunned breath. It seemed impossible, yet everything within her urged her to believe.

'There's only one woman I want, Aurélie.' His words throbbed with a need that matched the primal pull and drag inside her own body.

Yet he made no move to meet her halfway.

She breathed deep, inhaling that tantalising male scent of clean skin, fresh air and spice.

'Then what's holding you back?'

He knew she wanted him. She hadn't let out a peep of complaint yesterday when he'd swept her into his arms to take her to bed. Yet now, frustratingly, she sensed a barrier between them.

His frown deepened. 'I'm trying not to take anything for granted. Because if I touch you again, there'll be no stopping. No time for second thoughts.' Lucien drew a breath that made his chest expand.

Aurélie had never heard or seen anything as powerfully arousing as Lucien, standing before her, warning he'd reached the limit of self-control. He made her feel confident and strong. Made her feel wanted and cherished. Even if it was only sex. She didn't make the mistake of thinking the attraction Lucien felt was more than physical.

But at this minute that didn't matter.

She stepped up and planted her palm on his shirt,

pressing against the solid muscle that protected his drumming heart.

For a second he stood still, then he took her other hand and pressed her palm against him, right where the hard ridge of his erection tested the limit of his tailoring. His eyes narrowed as he watched her, waiting for her reaction.

Desire crested as she curled her hand against him. Aurélie's inner muscles clenched and other muscles softened. Liquid heat spilled between her legs as her skin drew tight and her nipples puckered.

Lucien shuddered when she moved her hand against him. A pulse throbbed as he clenched his jaw.

She opened her mouth to say his name but the word stalled on her tongue as he moved his big hand between her thighs, cupping her hard.

Her reaction was instantaneous, a jerky buck forward into his touch. A clenching of fingers, one hand tearing at his shirt, the other at his trousers.

Aurélie heard an unfamiliar shushing sound and belatedly realised it was her breath, chugging into constricted lungs.

A second later there was no air between them. Their mouths fused, lips and tongues sliding together, seeking, urging, demanding. It was every bit as glorious as she remembered.

Before she could undo his clothes, Lucien pulled her T-shirt high, urging her arms up so he could slide it free. Air kissed her bare flesh as he dragged her bra off.

Another *shush* of breath. This time Lucien's, as he looked down at her. Aurélie's breasts felt heavy, tingling with the weight of his stare.

He swallowed hard. Seconds later he knelt before her, feasting on her breast, kneading the other till she cried out and arched back as sparks of fire showered inside her.

Aurélie shivered, her legs unsteady, only able to stand because of her grip on Lucien. One hand dug into his shoulder and the other held his head to her. She didn't ever want to let him go.

She shivered voluptuously as the fire inside whirled to a conflagration that threatened to consume her.

'No more.' It was a raw gasp and he didn't hear. Aurélie had to push at those hard shoulders till he withdrew just enough to survey her with eyes that looked blank with heat.

'Please.' She fumbled at his collar. 'I need you inside me.'

She felt the heavy pound of her heart against her ribs, heard the rasp of rough breathing. Moments later Lucien was rolling the last of her clothes down her hips to her thighs. His eyes held hers, even as he shoved the clingy material down to her ankles and she stepped free.

Aurélie had only managed to undo a couple of his shirt buttons. Lucien was more efficient. He simply gripped the open neck of his shirt and pulled. Seconds later he tossed the torn cotton to the floor and rose before her, kicking off his shoes and stripping his socks. He straightened and she had a perfect view of his sculpted torso. She heard the hiss of his zip, the sound of his trousers landing on the floor as she leaned in and kissed his bare chest.

Heaven!

Almost as heavenly as his arms wrapping around her, drawing her close so they touched all the way down their bodies.

Her breath came in sharp little bursts that didn't fill her lungs. Lucien was against her, naked and wanting, and it was better even than she'd imagined. She remembered the bliss of their night together but this was different. This was urgent and desperate, as if two months apart had turned attraction into need, desire into craving.

Lucien wrapped his arms around her, lifting her off her feet. Seconds later he sank down onto the edge of the bed with her cradled close, her knees splaying on either side of his hips so she sat astride him, breasts to chest, his erection hard against her abdomen. She wriggled and he gasped out an oath under his breath.

Warm hands on her hips urged her up onto her knees, her breasts sliding against his chest. Aurélie's eyes shut as she battled the overload of exquisite sensations. But not for long. This was too good to miss a second.

When she opened them Lucien's bright gaze snared hers. For a second neither moved. She felt his heavy pulse, the humid waft of his breath on her lips, the intense heat of his hard body.

The sense of fulfilment as if her body and even her soul had been waiting for this moment.

As his fingers tightened on her hips she slowly sank, this time nudging the head of his erection. For a microsecond they both stopped breathing, until staying still was no longer an option.

Aurélie slid down, centimetre by slow centimetre until it felt as if Lucien was lodged right at her heart. The feeling was wondrous. So wondrous she shuddered at the twin sensations of his eyes eating her up and his body completing hers.

He might let her set the pace but she sensed what it cost him to exert such tight control. His big body was taut and trembling with the effort of restraint. That in turn made the moment more piquant, her own response more acute.

'More,' Lucien demanded in a deliciously deep voice that growled across her bare flesh.

Aurélie was about to say that he already filled her completely, when his hand covered her breast, kneading and gently squeezing. She gasped, arching back, eyes closed, as a ripple of ecstasy took her.

She was so close. She wasn't sure she could move. Except Lucien was right. She wanted more too. Anchoring herself on his shoulders, she rose, luxuriating in the slide of their bodies, then sank again, a little harder, a little faster.

Then again and again.

Inside the fire built to a conflagration that threatened to consume her. She told herself she couldn't give in to it yet. They'd only just started and—

Thought died as he slid his thumb down through damp curls to press that sensitive nub at the centre of her sex.

There was a roaring sound, as if the world caught alight. She saw flames reflected in Lucien's eyes as they reached up to engulf her.

Aurélie was swept in a tornado of fire and light. And pleasure, such pleasure.

She heard a high, keening sound, felt the rush of blood and the power as they arched together. Then came something she'd never experienced before, since in the past they'd used condoms. Lucien's deep groan of release heralded his body's quickening and his seed pulsed into her.

It felt…profound.

She and Lucien had already made a baby so this feeling that they shared something unique didn't make sense.

Yet as she collapsed against his shoulder, riding the jerky motions of his powerful body, Aurélie smiled. It felt as if she and Lucien experienced the most profound link a man and woman could. A link that was physical, but so much more too. A link that bound them irrevocably.

CHAPTER TWELVE

LUCIEN WOKE TO a feeling of calm and well-being. There was no buzz in his brain, reminding him of the people relying on him, the work he had to do, his schedule and expectations.

Instead there was warmth and…cosiness.

He stretched, arching his back, and instantly stopped as he registered the warm, feminine body in his embrace. One arm was stretched beneath Aurélie and the other wrapped around the curve of her waist. He lay on his side, spooned behind her. That fresh hint of flowers teased his nostrils and when he bent closer, soft curls caressed his mouth.

He inhaled deeply, unable to resist.

Memories flooded of last night. Of the incredible rapture he'd found with her. The release and sense of utter rightness had confirmed he and Ilsa had done the right thing, ending their betrothal.

Aurélie even made him feel better about the way he tackled the task of kingship. Her words about Vallort being lucky to have him might have been naïve but they'd been a welcome change after months fretting that he wasn't ready for the role.

With her everything was simpler, despite the complications in the outside world.

Lucien felt once more that stillness, as of time stopping, while they were together. As if they were somewhere unaffected by the world rushing past.

He'd experienced it the night they'd met. She'd grounded him when the depth of his grief overwhelmed him.

He felt that sensation again now. He had no name for it. Could only assume it was a blend of supercharged attraction melded with understanding. Now that bond was strengthened by their child.

That had to explain the intensity of what they'd shared last night. The explosive ecstasy. When he'd finally come back to himself it felt as if he'd broken apart and the pieces had been put back together to make a new Lucien. Someone familiar but not quite the same as before.

Renewed. That was how he'd felt. Still felt.

These last couple of months had been an emotional strain and an enormous challenge. He'd grown up with the royal family, knew how it functioned, but had never expected to step into Justin's shoes.

Leading a nation racked by the deaths of not one but two beloved figures, proving himself and coming to grips with new responsibilities, had been his total focus.

Now that focus had shifted.

He stifled a grin, acknowledging his hard-on pressed against Aurélie's soft derrière. Imagining the ecstasy of losing himself in her lush warmth. But she was sleeping and she needed rest. He'd seen how stressed she was and how weary. Morning sickness had taken its toll.

With Aurélie desire was a constant. It had tortured him through the days when he was still caught in a dynastic betrothal but lusted after this gorgeous redhead. It had almost undone him when he'd tried to use logic to persuade her to stay.

Lucien tried and failed to repress the need to slide his erection against her warm curves. He bit his lip, forcing back a sigh of raw pleasure.

'You're awake.'

Lucien's eyes snapped open, taking in the pale light of dawn. 'Sorry,' he murmured. 'I didn't mean to wake you.' But now she was awake he fitted her more closely against him, fanning out his fingers across the silky skin of her abdomen. Excitement shot through him. His child was in there. Tiny, vulnerable, but alive.

His grin widened. This time it had nothing to do with sex. Or not as much, he corrected, as Aurélie moved, hips twitching in a shuffle that teased his tight groin.

'I've been awake for a while.'

Lucien's grin faded as he tried to read her tone. Was it pensive? Distracted? Had she lain there thinking through her list of objections to marriage?

His mouth firmed. Whatever it took, Aurélie would marry him, and soon.

'How are you feeling?' He glanced past the undrawn curtains to where the sky pinkened around the peak on the opposite side of the valley. 'Any morning sickness?'

She shook her head, her hair tickling him. 'Not at all, surprisingly. Not yet, anyway.'

Lucien heard a world of weariness in her tone. Despite the dictates of his body, it reminded him of how tough things were for her at the moment.

Reluctantly he lifted his hand from her warm flesh. 'I'll go and let you catch up on sleep.' He clenched his jaw, preparing to move away, despite an internal howl of protest.

Her hand on his stopped him. She planted his palm on her hip as she twisted a little, looking over her shoulder.

The movement of her buttocks against his erection made the breath hiss between his gritted teeth. Her rich brown gaze met his and it was as if it had a direct line to his libido. Try as he might, he couldn't prevent the throb of his arousal against her.

Aurélie's lips twitched. 'You're a morning person.'

He shrugged. His throat dried with the effort it took to hold still. If her lush body wasn't temptation enough, that almost-smile shredded his resolve to give her space.

'So am I. Usually.'

He nodded. 'I understand.' Even if she wasn't nauseous, she was probably fragile in the morning. She wouldn't want…

His heart hit his ribs as she pulled his hand up to cover her breast. Automatically his fingers closed around her ripe curves. Riper, surely, than before?

Lucien nuzzled her neck, brushing away wavy locks, then gently bit down at the spot where her shoulder curved up to her neck.

'Ah!' She arched, her derrière pushing back hard. Pleasure scudded through him.

'You like that?' He sounded smug and didn't care. He liked it when Aurélie forgot to argue and throw up obstructions. When she was responsive and downright needy. 'When we're married we can do this as often as you like. And more, much more.'

Gently he pinched her nipple, feeling her shudder of response and the rolling wave of excitement that made her undulate against him. He pushed his knee up high between her legs. Her choked moan was music to his ears.

'*When*, not *if*?' she gasped. 'You take a lot for granted.'

'You know it's the best option.' He kissed her neck, breathing in the scent of spring and needy woman. 'Best for our baby.' He slid his hand to her belly, feeling that surge of excitement over his child growing there. 'Best for us too, Aurélie. I promise you won't regret it.'

On the words he moved his hand to the downy hair at the juncture of her thighs, slipping through damp folds to the slick heat at her core.

A shudder erupted. From her or him? Either way, feeling her readiness for sex, hearing her laboured breaths, made him harder than ever.

Yet Lucien understood the art of negotiation. Reluctantly he lifted his hand and withdrew his knee from between her thighs. It was torture, since Aurélie wasn't the only one straining for completion.

'Lucien!' She grabbed his hand and pulled it towards her, but her strength was no match for his. 'Why did you stop?' It sounded like a sob.

'I'm waiting for you to say yes.'

'You *know* I want you!' She sounded petulant. Lucien imagined her pouting mouth and, despite his determination to make her wait, couldn't stop the tilt of his hips that brought him into delicious friction with her bare rump.

'Yes to marriage, Aurélie.'

She stilled. He heard her sigh. He was tempted to use his hands and mouth to tease her into submission but this was important. Instead he waited, willing her to see sense.

'I...'

'Yes?' He couldn't help himself; he planted his hand at her waist, his fingers spanning her ribcage, sliding along smooth, warm skin.

'It would be disastrous. A huge scandal.'

'I didn't take you for a coward, Aurélie. I don't care about scandal. I care about you and the baby. About us.'

He waited, throat dry and pulse too fast.

Then she sighed. 'On one condition.'

Even now she didn't make this simple. How easy he'd had it with previous lovers, who'd agreed with whatever he wanted. But that was one of the things that set Aurélie apart. She was her own woman. He liked that. Most of the time.

'Name it.'

'We don't announce it yet. I need time to prepare.'

'Agreed.' He knew, better than most, how taxing the transition to royalty could be. For Aurélie, brought up in another country, not knowing Vallort or him very well, it was much more difficult. She was right, the fallout when the press discovered he was marrying his pregnant lover—

'Then yes.'

She didn't sound like a woman who'd agreed to the deal of a lifetime. Wealth, status, hot sex, a stable home for their child…

Lucien leaned over her shoulder, turning her face up with his fingers. Their eyes met and emotion smacked him low in the belly. Aurélie didn't look feisty or argumentative. She looked lost, those big eyes anxious in her pale face.

Tenderness welled up within him. A need to reassure. He wanted to tell her he'd stand by her through whatever came, but didn't want to dwell on anything that would increase her doubts. For she was right, there were tough times ahead.

'Thank you, Aurélie. You honour me.'

Her crooked smile carved a trench through his gut. She still had doubts and he hated seeing her worried.

'Then distract me from what I've agreed to. Make love to me, Lucien.'

As if he needed urging.

He made to pull away and settle above her, but she shook her head. 'Like this.'

Lucien pressed his mouth to her shoulder. 'Any way you want, Aurélie.'

'Is that a promise?' Laughter lurked in her eyes. And was that excitement? The sombre mood dissipated as abruptly as it had descended.

'Count on it.' Slowly, he settled against her back, thigh between her legs, parting them. He nudged the slick folds waiting for him. Thinking about it blasted his willpower to smithereens. Especially as, before he could do it himself, her slim hand was there, guiding him, and he had to bite back a growl of warning.

Was it the feel of their almost joined bodies that threatened to send him over the edge? Or the new understanding they shared? Even simply watching the erotic excitement flush Aurélie's skin made this special.

Whatever the reason, taking this slow was going to be more difficult than ever. They'd barely started but Lucien knew this for the best sex of his life. So far.

Slowly, every muscle straining at the effort at control, he pushed up into honeyed heat.

Aurélie's eyelashes fluttered and her mouth opened on a sigh of satisfaction that spurred him on. Inching forward, drawing out the sensations, Lucien felt the enormity of the moment. Joining himself with the woman who'd be his mate for life.

'More.' She licked her lips and he pushed the rest of the way in a hard, uncontrolled thrust, stars exploding across his vision.

Lucien shut his eyes, searching for restraint. Maybe if he focused on the new laws waiting for his consent... Or the intricacies of the new trade deal.

It was no good. They were both too close. He felt Aurélie's excitement in the tiny rotations of her pelvis as she pressed back against him, heard it in her tantalising moan of pleasure.

He brushed his hand across her peaked nipples, enjoying her jerk of response and capitalising on it with another easy thrust. Then temptation triumphed. Vowing to take it slow next time, he cupped her sex then slid his finger across—

'Lucien!'

That was all it took.

Hand pressing hard on his, as if afraid he'd stop caressing her, or perhaps needing to cling on, Aurélie shattered. He felt the tremors build in force, her muscles drawing hard, milking him till he exploded in stunning climax.

The waves of ecstasy went on and on.

When Lucien's brain rejoined his body he realised that, like every time last night and on that night months ago, it felt as if he'd just experienced the most stunning sexual experience of his life. Yet each time it got better. His mind boggled at the possibilities.

As their sated bodies sank together in the remnants of bliss, he congratulated himself. Marriage to Aurélie might provoke gossip and even scandal. But the compensations would be spectacular.

When Aurélie woke the bed was empty. There was a dent in the other pillow and the sheets were rumpled, though the bedcover had been pulled up neatly to her shoulders.

As if Lucien had straightened the bedding so she was warm and cosy. She stretched, her body instantly reminding her that last night had been no ordinary night. She and Lucien had had sex multiple times and each time it had felt as if he'd opened a door to heaven.

She smiled as she shuffled higher in the bed, plumping up the pillows.

A sudden swooping dive in her stomach sliced through her rose-tinted thoughts. Aurélie breathed slowly out through her mouth, trying not to move too much as she reached for the glass of water on her bedside table. Her stomach roiled as she took a small sip. She waited, trying to assess if the morning sickness would increase or lessen. Another cautious sip.

She was congratulating herself that it appeared to be easing when a rolling tide of nausea rose higher.

She slammed the glass down and thrust back the covers, hurrying across the carpet to the lavish en suite bathroom.

So much for her post-coital glow. The woman staring at her from the mirror had parchment-pale skin and a bruised look under her eyes. Her hair was wild and so were her eyes as she fought the inevitable.

Fought and lost.

Seconds later she was hunched, retching over the toilet, wishing she hadn't eaten last night because then she'd have nothing to bring up. Her arms shook and her eyes watered at each violent spasm. Even her skin was taut and clammy. All she could do was hang on and ride the wave of misery.

Then, out of nowhere, warmth encompassed her shivering body. Callused fingers pulled her hair back, anchoring it behind her ears, and she gave an unsteady nod of thanks.

Lucien. The heat of his hard-packed muscles and the tenderness of his skimming touch were so familiar.

She had a moment to wish he hadn't found her like this.

When they'd been in bed together she'd felt like a sex goddess. Now she had all the charm of a dishrag. Then another bout of sickness hit and pride disappeared. She was simply grateful for his support, one arm carefully bracing her while with the other he blotted her forehead with a damp cloth.

When the wave passed she leant back against him, letting him take her weight. Silently he wiped her face, the dampness reviving her enough to open her eyes.

'Thank you. I think it's over now.'

'You want to get up?'

Aurélie nodded, telling herself that in another second she'd have the energy to rise.

Before she could try, Lucien tossed the washcloth into the basin and scooped her up against him. For a second the world tilted and she gasped, fearing the worst. But, as if he read her thoughts, Lucien stood still, waiting till she nodded before taking her back to the bed.

Installed there, catching the V of concern furrowing his brow, she felt self-conscious.

'Sorry. That can't have been nice for you.'

'You're apologising for your morning sickness?' He sat beside her and reached for her hand, threading his fingers through hers. 'I'm just glad I could help. It's rotten that you have to go through this on top of the shock of finding yourself pregnant.'

Aurélie shot him a startled look.

'What's wrong?'

It should worry her that Lucien read her so easily, but she couldn't bring herself to stress about it now. He was right. She still felt too fragile.

'Nothing. It's…' She paused and shrugged. 'Whenever my stepmother was sick during pregnancy my father made a point of leaving the house.

He didn't like to be around illness.' It had been left to Aurélie to do whatever was necessary to help her stepmother and look after the boys. It had become a habit over the years till she'd become the one responsible for all the household chores. Her stepmother had got used to relying on Aurélie and never bothered teaching her sons to share the workload. 'I'm not used to men who are so…domesticated.'

Or to anyone caring for *her*. Most of her life she'd felt almost invisible, taken for granted like a piece of furniture. Aurélie couldn't remember the last time anyone in her family had noticed her enough to consider what *she* needed, much less supported her.

Lucien's mouth hooked up, turning his frown into a wry, far too attractive smile. 'You make me sound like a tabby cat.'

'Hardly.' Her gaze dropped to the wide straight line of his shoulders, skating across to the open top button of his pristine business shirt and lower to that hard torso she could snuggle against all day. Lucien had all the power and lethal athleticism of a predatory big cat, despite the way he made her purr.

'Aurélie, you're carrying all the burden of this baby right now. The least I can do is help where I can.' His stare held hers and she felt something inside ease and soften. 'Speaking of which, I went to get you biscuits and ginger tea. I'm told ginger is good to prevent nausea. And you need to keep up your fluids.'

His words settled behind her breastbone, snug and comforting, and she drew a deep, unfettered breath. Was she really so besotted, so needy, that Lucien's practical concern affected her?

It seemed so. She felt again that abrupt spike of emotion and vulnerability she'd experienced before when he was kind.

Lucien reached for the tray he'd put beside the bed. Had the doctor recommended this or had Lucien taken time to enquire about possible remedies?

Either way, that melting sensation quickened at the sight of him pouring a small cup of fragrant, pale liquid with as much concentration as if he were handling a rare antique.

His expression was serious as he held it out to her and watched her take a sip. Aurélie held her breath, wondering if she'd be making another undignified bolt to the bathroom, but this time her stomach didn't rebel.

'Lovely,' she sighed. And it was. Not just the tea, but the way he made her feel.

Cherished. Again that word sprang into her mind. Though she understood Lucien was making the best of a bad situation. Last night, in the throes of passion, she could be excused thinking he really cared. But now, in the light of day, she couldn't let herself be swept away by foolish imaginings.

She was taking another sip when Lucien spoke.

'About your stipulation. About needing more time before we announce our wedding.' He paused as if waiting to make sure he had her attention. 'We need to agree a timeline. There's a lot to organise.'

Aurélie nodded, ignoring the dragging sensation inside. *Disappointment.*

Naturally Lucien needed a timeline. Their marriage would be as practical as his arrangement with Ilsa. They were doing this for the sake of their baby and to secure the royal succession. The feeling of being cherished evaporated.

'I want to be married well before the baby arrives.'

Again she nodded, feeling like a puppet whose strings were being pulled by a master. Of course he wanted to marry before the birth. He wanted a legitimate heir.

Because he was royal and such things mattered.

'If we keep it very simple and small…' Aurélie stopped as Lucien shook his head.

'Simple and small won't be possible.' As if reading her horror he went on quickly. 'We can tailor it as much as possible to suit your preferences, but this won't be a hole-and-corner event. We need to show the world that you're a suitable consort. And we need to give the people of Vallort a chance to share the celebration.' His expression changed, a flicker of something that looked like pain dimming his eyes. 'Something joyous after all the grief.'

Aurélie swallowed, forcing down her automatic protest. She'd been about to fight him on this. The thought of a big wedding full of pomp, with her at its centre, an imposter pretending to be a royal princess, made her nauseous. And that had nothing to do with morning sickness.

Everyone would see this was a sham, that *she* was a sham.

But that haunted look in Lucien's eyes stopped her. Aurélie forced herself to take another sip of tea. It didn't taste as good as before.

'A royal wedding takes lots of planning.'

'You mean you don't want to wait to announce our engagement.' Her voice sounded as dull as the leaden weight sitting in her stomach.

'I agreed to give you time, Aurélie.' He paused, mouth compressing. 'But there are limits.'

'Have you thought about what you're asking me to do?' Her voice rose unsteadily and she clamped her teeth on her bottom lip, not liking the thready note of panic she heard.

'I have.' His gaze held hers and, surprisingly, she felt that tremor of distress settle. 'Don't forget I've come into this role unexpectedly too.'

'But you were brought up royal, even if you never expected to inherit. You know how it all works.' She lifted her chin to indicate their surroundings. 'You grew up in a castle! I grew up in a cramped flat in a working-class neighbourhood.'

He covered the hand that wasn't holding the teacup. Absurdly, Lucien's touch eased her jittery pulse. When she had spare time to think on that,

Aurélie knew it would be yet another thing to disturb her.

'Which means I can help you. I've made a list of people who can bring you up to speed on what you need to know.'

Aurélie reached across to put her cup down, her mouth firming. She imagined a schedule of tutors trying and failing to turn a commoner into a queen. Would she have to practise deportment, walking with a heavy book on her head? Learn to curtsey? Have a crash course in politics?

She moistened dry lips, about to tell him it was too overwhelming.

'Isn't it worth it, for the sake of our child?'

Aurélie sagged back against her pillows. Mere days ago she'd planned on returning to France and raising this baby alone. She told herself that was still possible.

Except it wasn't.

Not because she wanted her child to inherit a throne. Not because she wanted to be Queen. But because she recognised Lucien's care for this baby and understood he would love it too. That was too precious to ignore.

Lucien was determined and that would make a huge difference to their baby. It would have a father who fought for it in every way that counted.

Unlike her father. Who'd ignored her, except as an unpaid drudge.

If they married she'd secure a family for her

child, the chance to study as she'd dreamed, plus she'd be with Lucien...

'Aurélie?'

Her breath faltered as she met Lucien's probing stare. Reluctantly she answered. 'Yes, it's worth it.'

Was that relief that made his shoulders drop while hers tightened?

'Give me three weeks before you make the announcement. They say the first twelve are when there's most danger of complications.' She stopped, trying not to think about the possibility of miscarriage.

'Three weeks then.' Lucien smiled and raised her hand to kiss it. But strangely Aurélie felt no shiver of sensual awareness. Because all his delight was for the baby. This wedding was to secure its birthright.

She should be used to it now. Since her mother died, she'd never been more than a convenience to anyone. She'd never been treasured or loved. Never valued for herself.

Aurélie set her jaw and told herself it didn't matter.

Lucien was marrying her for their baby's sake and she was doing the same. That was what counted.

She ignored the crumbling feeling inside. As if the futile imaginings she'd begun to spin around this man during last night's passion cracked and disintegrated.

CHAPTER THIRTEEN

'HIS MAJESTY IS on the phone, mademoiselle.'

The housekeeper waited in the doorway as Aurélie approached from the woodland path, quickening her step.

In the five days since she'd arrived at the castle her morning sickness had become just that, hitting her only in the morning. She'd got into the habit of heading out for a walk mid-morning, enjoying the clear air and fairyland beauty of green dells and deep forest. The weather had improved, the sun shining and the temperature rising.

Aurélie had a full afternoon ahead, with a tutor coming to teach her about the government, administration and politics of Vallort. Maybe he'd had to cancel…

She was fascinated by Lucien's country, but studying to become a queen left her unsettled and doubtful.

'Thank you.'

The housekeeper smiled as she handed over the phone and disappeared inside the castle.

A *castle*. Aurélie was staying in a castle. She was the King's lover and would be mother of a future monarch. Yet again the unreality of her situation sideswiped her.

'Aurélie? Are you there?'

There it was. The deep-seated sizzle that came

whenever she heard Lucien's voice. She'd hoped it would abate—the strange magic when she heard his voice purr the syllables of her name. But still she was in thrall. Five days as Lucien's lover, sharing his bed, and the cosy evening hours when they shut the world out, and the magic ensnared her more strongly than ever.

'I'm here, Lucien.' Aurélie turned to look down the valley to the city where he was.

She didn't have time for magic. If she wasn't careful she'd start imagining there was more between them than sexual attraction and an unplanned pregnancy.

'What is it? You sound different. Are you okay?'

The man was too perceptive. Of course she wasn't okay. She was too fond of him, too caught up in what he made her feel. Things could only end in tears if she let herself believe he cared for her as anything other than his baby's mother.

'I'm fine. I've been for a walk and feel better for it.'

'You're not sick?' Concern tinged his voice and she couldn't stop a flare of delight that he cared.

Because you're carrying his child. Remember?

'No, I'm okay.' She paused, realising how unusual it was for him to call during work hours. 'What is it, Lucien? Is everything all right there?'

This week had been tough on him, though Lucien refused to burden her with details. When he arrived home each evening, there was no mistaking the strain he tried to mask.

Fortunately they found ways to relieve that strain…

'You're worried about me?'

Aurélie couldn't tell if that was hope in his voice or curiosity. But it wouldn't do to let him know exactly how much she felt for him. As it was, parting each day was ridiculously difficult.

Because of pregnancy hormones or something else?

'You have an enormous workload and you're facing tremendous pressure.'

Yet just yesterday he'd carved out a couple of hours to take her to a charming mountain inn for lunch. What made the date special wasn't a romantic rendezvous, but that he'd invited his closest friends to meet her, introducing her as 'special to me' but not mentioning her pregnancy.

Aurélie was stunned by his generosity, drawing her firmly into that warm, intimate circle with no caveats, just open-hearted acceptance.

As if she *were* special.

Her own circle of friends had broken when some had moved away and others had grown distant as she'd devoted herself to longer hours working at home and the restaurant.

Aurélie had been nervous yesterday, expecting a backlash over the broken engagement. But Lucien's friends had been welcoming. There'd been no judgement, though she guessed they were curious. They'd set her at ease and she'd enjoyed herself enormously.

'Don't worry about me, Aurélie. It's nothing I can't handle. You concentrate on resting.' It was a familiar refrain, as if her bouts of sickness really worried him.

'You only want me to rest so I'm ready to learn about politics and parliamentary processes.'

He huffed a laugh that rippled like sunshine over her skin. 'That's only for one afternoon. Surely you can spare the time. Besides, I was ringing to tell you I've arranged something a lot more appealing. A couple of things, actually.'

Aurélie's hand tightened on the receiver. 'I don't need treats, Lucien. I totally get that this is stuff I need to understand if I stay here.'

Silence lengthened. She'd snapped the words out like an ungrateful harridan. She'd said *if* she stayed, though she'd already agreed to marry him.

Yet every time she thought of the future Lucien planned she felt nervous and worried.

'I'm sorry, Lucien. I'm a little…'

Out of my depth?

Petrified I'm falling in love with you?

Aurélie drew in a slow breath. 'What did you want to tell me?'

'You'll have two more visitors this afternoon.' His tone was unreadable and for some reason that was worse than hearing anger or disappointment.

'A stylist will visit straight after lunch with a selection of clothes for you to choose from. I want you to feel comfortable that you have something appropriate for any occasion.'

Aurélie was about to object, then stopped. He was right. She had only a handful of outfits here. Even if she had access to all her clothes she had nothing suitable to wear in royal circles.

'No complaints?'

Her mouth twisted ruefully. 'You know me too well.'

'I know you're independent and you don't like being beholden, but—'

'It's okay, Lucien. I can see the wisdom of having the right clothes.'

Though accepting them felt a step closer to the future that felt so unreal. She'd already agreed, yet she baulked at the idea. Surely his people would never accept her. Aurélie bit her lip and dragged her gaze from the city in the distance to the calming green of the forest.

'And the other thing you've arranged?'

If it was deportment classes she'd just have to grin and bear it.

'You have a half hour lesson at five-thirty with a piano tutor.'

'Sorry?' She couldn't have heard right.

'You said you'd always wanted to learn the piano.' He paused and when he spoke again his voice dragged low across her senses. 'I thought it might make the crash course on being a royal easier if you had something fun to look forward to, like music lessons.'

Aurélie opened her mouth then closed it again. She blinked as the forest greens blurred.

'I…' She swallowed hard, a sharp knot of emotion scraping her throat then raking down into her chest. 'Thank you, Lucien, that's…' Her throat closed again.

'Aurélie?' His voice sharpened. 'I thought you'd be happy.'

She pressed a hand to her breastbone, trying to hold in the riot of feelings. Her heart hammered and her chest felt too full.

'I am…happy. Thank you. That's very thoughtful.' She swallowed. 'I need to go now. Sorry.'

Disconnecting the call, she leaned against the doorway, overwhelmed. Hadn't she known from the first that Lucien made her feel too much?

This confirmed it. His gift of piano lessons was thoughtful and well meant. It was the nicest thing anyone had done for her in…well, as long as she could recall. Not since her mother had anyone taken time to do anything special for her.

The fact that Lucien remembered her desire to play the piano, that he'd thought about it in the midst of the pressures he faced and then acted on it, because he wanted to make her happy…

Beneath her palm her heart thundered.

Through the tall trees, beams of sunlight shone; she was transfixed by their brightness.

That was how she felt inside. Burning bright.

Because she couldn't pretend any longer. She'd fallen in love with Lucien. His kindness as much as his passion undid her.

Somehow she had to work out a way to marry him, have his baby and live with him, play the part of his Queen, and never betray her feelings for him.

'His Majesty said you like bright colours,' the stylist said, smiling, as she wheeled in several racks of clothes.

Which proved again that Lucien paid attention. Aurélie's heart gave a fluttery thump, like it had when he'd told her about the piano lessons. Ridiculous to feel wobbly inside. Simply because he'd noticed *her*, thought about her preferences.

It made her feel *cared for*. Something she wasn't used to.

Aurélie loved colour, including some yellows and deep pinks that redheads were supposedly not meant to wear. Yet she was surprised he'd paid attention. Or surprised he'd remembered to mention the fact. She'd imagined him telling his secretary to make sure she had suitable clothes and then turning back to other business.

The stylist pulled the cover off the first rack and Aurélie sucked in a stunned breath.

The light caught jewel colours that gleamed rich

and inviting, wonderful dresses that even she could tell were haute couture.

She couldn't resist reaching out to finger the sleeve of a jade-green dress, its silk as fine as a butterfly's wing. The slippery satin of an evening gown in deep amethyst. A halter-neck in an amber shade that reminded her of Lucien's eyes.

'It helped that I knew about your fabulous colouring.' The woman smiled as she uncovered another rack. This one was filled with trousers and jackets, including a long, stylish coat of cobalt blue wool that Aurélie couldn't take her eyes off.

'Yes, you'd look terrific in that. The fitted style would make the most of your slim figure.'

Aurélie's hand dropped. Not slim for long. How far into her pregnancy would she develop a baby bump?

'I don't need too much. Just a few things for the moment.'

The stylist nodded and smiled but immediately explained that a full wardrobe had been ordered. 'Perhaps if we start on what you're going to need in the next week or two, then see how we go?' She ran an expert eye over Aurélie, then back to the racks. 'Tonight, for instance, you'll want something special.'

'Tonight?'

'For the opening of that new photographic exhibition people are talking about.' Seeing Aurélie's blank look, she went on, curiosity evident. 'I was supposed to tell you to be ready at eight. Apparently there was some problem getting the message to you earlier.'

Probably because Aurélie had hung up on Lucien before he could tell her. Guiltily she bit her lip.

Had he realised she'd felt undone by his kindness, or did he think her still in a snit over the 'royal' tutorials he'd arranged?

Quickly Aurélie nodded, pretending she'd known about the opening. It must be the one she'd heard about yesterday. One of Lucien's good friends was a professional photographer. His wife, a bank executive, had spoken about this new exhibition and how he'd almost broken his neck climbing a glacier at dawn to get the right shot. By the time they'd finished describing some of his more outrageous adventures in search of the perfect photo, Aurélie had been relaxed and laughing with the rest of them.

Now, though, she faced the prospect of deciding what to wear for a gala opening. She was torn between eagerness at seeing the exhibition and Lucien's friends, and dismay at accompanying him in public. Surely it was too soon after his broken engagement?

'Do you have any suggestions for tonight?'

The stylist put her head to one side. 'Nothing too formal, of course.' She moved away from the full-length dresses and Aurélie relaxed a little. 'But definitely something eye-catching. The opening is a high-profile event. Everyone who's anyone will be there.'

She reached for a cocktail length dress in bright aqua, shimmering with tiny beads.

'It's gorgeous.' Instinctively Aurélie moved closer then stopped herself. 'But I think something not so bright.'

'You'd look a million dollars in this style and the colour against your wonderful hair would turn every head.'

That was what Aurélie was afraid of. 'I think, for tonight, I'd rather not stand out from the crowd.'

She caught speculation in the other woman's eyes, then the stylist nodded her understanding.

'Society events can be a bit overwhelming if you're not used to them.' She didn't glance at Aurélie's jeans and cheap knitted top, but she'd no doubt sized them up in the first seconds of them meeting. 'Okay, something a little less bright, at least for tonight, yes?'

Aurélie's tight shoulders eased a little. 'Yes, that would be perfect.'

'How are you holding up?' Lucien lowered his voice and Aurélie felt it as a velvet caress across her shivery skin. That deep murmur reminded her of making love. Then his voice, roughened with arousal, would make her body sing as much as his touch and his hungry amber stare.

'I'm good.' Her smile was real, not like the fake

one she'd put on as they'd arrived at the gallery. 'I'm actually enjoying myself.'

Especially as no one had thrust out an accusing finger, pointing to her as an intruder who didn't belong. Though there *were* plenty of curious looks. The gala opening had attracted a glamorous crowd and Lucien hadn't left her side.

'I'm pleased.' His hand lingered at the small of her back, not quite touching, yet her skin warmed as if from direct contact.

Her heartbeat stilled for a moment as she caught satisfaction in Lucien's eyes and something more. Heat blossomed in her pelvis.

Aurélie heaved a deep breath, fighting excitement at his flagrantly possessive expression. But that only made her breasts rise against the midnight-blue silk of her dress and Lucien's gaze dropped to her bodice. Inevitably her nipples pebbled needily.

'Stop it,' she hissed. 'You're drawing attention to me.'

She'd been unable to resist the dress the stylist had suggested. Aurélie had assumed the darker colour and simple lines would help her blend into the background. She'd reckoned without the fact that standing beside the King meant she could never be in the background. Or that the silk's lustrous shine drew attention to the shape of her body. Had it clung so much when she'd tried it on this afternoon?

The almost grim line of Lucien's mouth turned

up in a rueful smile. 'Believe me, Aurélie, you don't need me to draw attention to you. You're doing that all by yourself. You look magnificent.'

She shook her head, trying not to react to his over-the-top praise.

'*Those* are magnificent.' She gestured towards the photographs on the black wall before them. Alpine scenes in deepest winter. 'Your friend is so talented. The light and shade on that frozen waterfall is amazing.'

'I agree. They're some of his best, and he'll be delighted to hear you say it.' His voice dropped. 'But you're changing the subject.'

Aurélie's chin jerked up. 'I don't need flattery, Lucien.'

But when she met his eyes he looked completely serious. 'You don't believe you look magnificent?'

She shot a quick look around and found that for once there was no one standing close. Yet instinctively she moved closer to a photo of tiny meadow flowers surrounding a mirror-surfaced mountain lake.

'So long as I look passable, I'll be happy.' She'd never mixed with people in couture fashion and jewels before. Never run the gauntlet of press photographers. It had been nerve-racking, though Lucien had thoughtfully arranged for them to arrive with the friends they'd met yesterday.

There it was again. Thoughtfulness.

Because he cared?

Or because he didn't want her spooked into changing her mind about staying?

Lucien listened to Aurélie chat with a German count and countess about kayaking.

They'd met in front of a stunning photo of a kayaker descending rapids in full flood. It turned out Aurélie had enjoyed the little kayaking she'd done years before with a friend, enough to unwind when the Count began talking of rapids and Eskimo rolls. Her eyes shone brightly and the tension that had stiffened her shoulders all evening evaporated.

He guessed it would return if she realised she was talking to the CEO of one of Europe's most prosperous banks or that his wife was a senior diplomat.

Lucien knew Aurélie felt out of place with the rich and powerful. If only he could convince her that the job of royalty was as much about protecting and serving ordinary citizens as it was about mingling with VIPs. But that was something she'd have to realise for herself over time.

If only she knew it, her down-to-earth freshness totally suited the Vallort royal family, which, for the last two generations at least, had focused on substance rather than pomp. As a royal, she'd spend as much time interacting with the general public as the privileged.

Another couple joined the group and Lucien watched, delighted, as Aurélie chatted easily. Her vivacity drawing more than one admiring glance. Once she forgot about social barriers and royalty she was fine.

More than fine.

Lucien spoke little and he realised how relaxing it was not to have to carry the whole burden of conversation. How good it felt to have a partner who could contribute and take her share of social interaction.

It wasn't something he'd considered when he'd insisted Aurélie marry him.

But lots of things weren't as he'd imagined then.

His feelings about Aurélie for a start.

It had been easy to decide that marriage was their only option. Because he refused to give up his child—his *family*.

But their relationship wasn't just about duty. Which was some compensation, since the scandal he dealt with now was nothing to the blast of attention they'd get when it was discovered she carried his child.

Nor was it simply protectiveness he felt. Nor even lust, though both were there, strong and easy to recognise.

What he felt for Aurélie…

Looking at her, vibrant and sexy, made his chest ache.

Unlike most women here she wore no jewellery except tiny stud earrings. Her deep blue dress was plain but it packed a punch he felt right to his groin.

Whenever he looked at her he imagined his hands following the contours of her luscious body.

She had no need of diamonds or gold to catch the eye. But as soon as he thought of her in jewels, his unruly mind conjured an image of her wearing some of the royal jewels. And nothing else.

His throat dried and his brain blurred so the bustle towards the exit took him by surprise. He looked at his watch. The event was ending.

Lucien drew Aurélie closer. 'Are you tired? If you prefer we could go straight home instead of to supper with the others.' He'd enlisted his friends' assistance to enter and leave together in the hope that any paparazzi wouldn't single Aurélie out for special attention. That would come soon enough but she was understandably skittish about the press.

Brilliant eyes met his as she gave him a stunning smile. The impact would have rocked a lesser man. His hand tightened on her elbow. It would be selfish to hope she'd opt to go straight to bed—

'I'd love to go to supper with your friends.' Aurélie lowered her voice. 'I've had such a lovely night I don't want it to end. I'd forgotten how much I like being with people.'

That reinforced his assessment of her personality. Her warmth as she'd chatted with customers that first night wasn't solely because it was her job. She was genuinely interested in them.

Then her forehead creased. 'Unless you'd rather not. You've had a long day.'

She was worried about *him* being tired? She was the one carrying their baby. A thought which turned him on as much as it evoked protectiveness. Now her concern was liquid warmth in his already overheated body.

'Oh, I think I've got enough energy for a little more *excitement* tonight.' His voice dropped as he took her hand, running his thumb across the centre of her palm and the sensitive skin of her wrist. Satisfaction surged at her shudder of response.

Her eyes glowed and her lips parted and Lucien cursed himself as a fool for playing this suggestive game as his arousal tightened his trousers.

'Come on, Aurélie. The others are ready.'

The group walked from the gallery half a block to a restaurant tucked into an old hotel renowned for exquisite and innovative food. The evening was convivial and they enjoyed the camaraderie of the group.

It was good to relax with friends, putting aside for a couple of hours the burdens of kingship. And when he draped his arm around the back of Aurélie's chair and she leaned closer he didn't even try to find a definition for the upswell of emotion that flowed hot and strong inside.

Even the photographers in the street failed to destroy his good humour.

And when they reached the castle tower where Aurélie had shared his bed for almost a week, his sense of well-being grew.

'I like your friends,' she said as she unpinned her hair and a froth of fiery waves cascaded around her shoulders.

'I'm glad. They like you too.' He pulled her in and bent his head, burying his face in that mass of lilac-scented waves. Aurélie smelled like spring. Could that be why he craved her so badly? Until she came he'd felt he faced endless winter.

His arms tightened, hauling her close. 'I love your hair.'

He felt a second's surprise at his choice of words. He wasn't a teenage girl who *loved* this or that. But it was true, he did love her hair. And her soft skin. And...

'Really? It's very bright. And I have to work to keep it under control. Pinning it up tonight took ages.'

Lucien drew back enough to meet her dark eyes. 'It's perfect. It's vibrant like you and I love the curls. Do you have to pin it up?'

'It looks tidier that way. More formal.'

He watched her chew her lip, something she hadn't done all evening.

Because they were talking, obliquely, about how royalty looked and she wasn't at ease with the idea of becoming a queen. The change from the confident woman earlier this evening made him pause.

Lucien straightened and slipped his hands down to capture hers, threading their fingers together.

'Start as you mean to go on.'

'Sorry?'

'It's something my uncle used to tell Justin. That when the time came for him to inherit the throne he should start as he meant to go on.' He paused, realising that for the first time he'd spoken of them without that awful catch in his chest. 'He said each new monarch had to forge his own way, make his own rules and be comfortable with his choices. He was all for moulding the job, as he called it, to suit changing circumstances and generations.'

'I don't understand.'

'It's natural you're overwhelmed by the idea of becoming royal. But in my family it's viewed as both an honourable obligation and a job. We're bound by it but each generation makes it their own.' He paused, realising how important this was and that he wasn't explaining clearly.

'For instance, I know you were concerned to-night was too soon to be seen in public with me. But I intend to be your husband. There's nothing to be gained by hiding you away from the press. I'm not ashamed of you or our baby.' Lucien felt his chest rise. 'Vallort, and the press, will grow accustomed to us being together. That's something I won't bend on.'

Aurélie regarded him seriously but Lucien wasn't sure she was convinced.

'If you want to wear your hair loose, do it. If you want to wear one of those cute ponytails—' her eyebrows shot up and he smiled '—then do it.' He shook his head. 'There are some things we can't change—the constitution and the laws of inheritance—but if anything, and I mean *anything* about the way we live our lives as royals bothers you, then tell me and we'll search for a compromise.'

Finally she nodded. 'Thank you. I like the idea of compromise and hearing some of the rules might be elastic. Maybe that way when I make a mistake it won't be a disaster.'

Lucien stroked his hands up to her shoulders, enjoying her sensual shiver. Deliberately he massaged her shoulders, feeling tense muscles loosen.

'We all make mistakes. Ask my staff. I've kept them busy since taking the throne. I still have a lot to learn.'

Her eyebrows rose and to his delight she slanted him a sultry smile. 'In some things. In others you're very proficient, Your Majesty.'

That was when he noticed her nipples thrusting against the silk of her dress. 'Proficient, eh? At what?'

He skimmed his hands down her bodice to cup her breasts. Her breath sighed out and her back arched as she pushed into his touch. Lucien had no idea if her responsiveness was due to pregnancy hormones or a naturally sensuous nature, but he loved Aurélie's eagerness for sex.

Another thing he loved about her.

He might tell himself marriage was the right thing to protect Aurélie and his baby, but he couldn't fool himself that he was motivated purely by duty. His feelings for her were far more complex.

'You know exactly what I mean,' she murmured, licking her lips.

And just like that she turned the tables on him. That pink tongue against those soft lips. The glorious bounty of her silk-clad breasts in his hands. The perfume of her skin—flowers and female arousal.

His groin hardened, heavy with blood rushing south.

'But practice makes perfect, don't you agree?' He bent to fit his mouth over one pert nipple and sucked hard. Hands clawed at his skull and her pelvis thrust into him.

'I think…' she gasped '…it's time to stop teasing and put your money where your mouth is.'

Lucien swallowed a chuckle of delight and proceeded to strip his lover bare. Then he took them both to a pinnacle of ecstasy that couldn't be, but seemed, even higher and more perfect than the ones they'd reached last night.

Each time with Aurélie seemed better than before.

And it wasn't just sex. Tonight, being in her company, enjoying her enjoyment, had been a delight.

Finally, well past midnight, they slumped together, sated and content. Blissfully unaware of the firestorm about to hit them.

CHAPTER FOURTEEN

LUCIEN STARED AT the headlines in the media report his office had sent through.

He'd known this was going to happen. He'd been prepared. Or he'd thought he was. Yet he felt nauseous.

Was this how Aurélie felt when morning sickness hit?

Aurélie. His mouth firmed and his gut clenched.

For most of his life the press had published positive stories about the Vallort royal family. True, there'd been speculation and shock about his broken engagement. But, if today's press reports were any indication, things had changed. Not so much for him, but for Aurélie.

A cold, hard sensation settled low inside. It was okay for him to talk about standing up to public opinion. Poor Aurélie hadn't asked for this and didn't deserve it.

He'd expected to bear the brunt of any negativity. He'd assumed she'd be painted as an innocent and he a serial seducer.

Which showed he'd never make a journalist.

A surge of rage pummelled him. He wanted to ring the editors and shout at them. Except that would be exactly the wrong thing to do. Instead he'd have to bury his ire and decide how to deal with this. His team had been developing a PR strategy but it needed work.

'You're still here! I thought you'd left.' Aurélie stood in the doorway wearing a new wrap of soft green. She looked like a woodland sprite with her wide eyes, pale skin and glowing hair cascading around her shoulders.

A sexy sprite, with that nipped-in waist and curves his hands itched to touch, even now when he wrestled with incandescent rage.

Lucien shoved the chair back from his desk. 'Something came up that the palace wanted me to see straight away.'

She moved further into his study, a symphony of soft curves and lithe lines that dried his brain despite the urgent need for action.

'Something bad.' It was a statement.

Lucien hesitated. His instinct was to shield her. Especially as it was his fault she faced this. If he'd been an ordinary citizen, not a king… But regrets were useless and Aurélie needed to know.

'There are reports about us.'

'Because we went out last night?' She refrained from saying *I told you so*. He'd been adamant that they shouldn't wait till he announced their engagement for Aurélie to appear in public. That had felt too much as if he were hiding a dirty secret, instead of presenting the woman who'd be his wife.

He spread his hands, palms up. 'And about our lunch the day before.'

'With your friends?' Her brow twitched as if her concern was about the intrusion into his friends' privacy.

'The press has had time to discover your name and nationality. They'll be digging for more now.'

Aurélie clutched the front of her robe with one hand, her chin going up. 'It was inevitable, I suppose.'

Regret was temporarily eclipsed by admiration. His woman had steel in her spine.

Lucien couldn't stop himself. He stepped in, wrapped an arm around her waist, plunged his hand into the thick mass of her glorious hair and kissed her full on the lips. Fire ignited as their lips fused. Their bodies aligned as the kiss deepened and Lucien was tempted to carry her back to bed.

But he couldn't be so selfish. He had to work with his staff to refine their PR strategy. To make things better for her.

Breathing heavily, he drew back enough to meet Aurélie's eyes.

'Is it really that bad?'

'It's not good. I'd suggest staying in the castle today. No one will bother you here.'

'I see.' Her gaze meshed with his. '*That* bad.'

Lucien shrugged, but his shoulders felt stiff. 'It will get better. I'm going now to meet with key staff about our media response.'

'What can I do?'

Once more it hit him that he'd struck gold with

this woman. They mightn't see eye to eye on everything but she was resolute and courageous. His baby would have a wonderful mother. His country would have a wonderful queen.

'Why are you smiling? I didn't say anything funny.'

She frowned and Lucien hurried to explain. 'It was a smile of approval, Aurélie.' He stroked the back of his hand down her cheek. Soft as a peach but she had a core of strength he could only admire. 'As for what you can do, rest up this morning. Don't worry about the press for now. You've got tutorials this afternoon and when I come back tonight we'll discuss how we're to deal with this. Okay?'

Slowly she nodded and Lucien felt a tiny bit of the weight lift from his shoulders. By tonight he'd be better placed to discuss concrete options with her.

'Walk me to the car?' He slid her arm through his and smiled when she pressed close.

What he and Aurélie shared might have begun unconventionally but there was something genuine and strong at its heart. They'd make this marriage work, despite what the world said.

Aurélie entered Lucien's study with a sense of trepidation. It was clear he didn't want her viewing the media reports. On the way to the car he'd reiterated that it would be better if she ignored the press today and they'd talk it through tonight.

It must be very bad.

She settled at his desk and lifted the lid of his laptop. He'd forgotten to shut it down and it opened immediately to a list of media stories. There were lots.

Aurélie hesitated. But she wasn't prying into state secrets. This was about her.

Last night Lucien's confidence in her, his support, had made her feel good about herself. As if, should she wish to, she could do anything she set her mind to. Just as her mother had told her when she was little. Just as she'd told herself time and again, as she'd fought against being ground down by her family's dismissiveness.

Breathing deep, she clicked on the attachment and saw story after story.

The first couple, from the local press in Vallort, were fairly mild. Curiosity over her identity. A couple of photos from last night. Reference to Lucien's broken engagement and speculation over her role in his life.

But then came the rest, from foreign press and social media. A barrage of blaring headlines that hit her like physical blows. A few painted Lucien as a callous playboy.

Ilsa Heartbroken as Lucien Flaunts New Lover!

And there was a photo of Ilsa looking stoic. But most focused on Aurélie. She read them with increasing horror.

Lucien's Red-Hot Redhead!

King Flaunts Mistress!

Tragic Ilsa Ousted by French Floozy!

Bile rose in her throat as the stories grew more and more lurid, with speculation that she'd seduced Lucien out of his betrothal with phenomenal sex. One sordid flight of fancy painted her as a whore who'd connived to get access to a royal fortune.

She slammed the laptop shut. Lucien was right. She didn't want to read this.

It could only get worse when they discovered he planned to marry her. That she carried his child.

Aurélie swallowed, battling nausea.

She was caught. Even if she broke her promise to marry him, the press would follow her. There'd be stories about her child, probably even more cruel ones, if she left Lucien and returned to France. The press would never go away. The stories would continue for years, about the King's child and Lucien's ex-lover.

She looked at her hands, clenched on the laptop. It made sense to stay.

But that wasn't why she'd remain.

She'd do it *because she loved Lucien.* Had fallen in love with him that first night, no matter how improbable that seemed.

Everything she'd learned about him since—his

honesty and sense of duty, his positivity and kindness, his wry sense of humour and camaraderie—just strengthened her feelings. Aurélie didn't want to leave him. She wanted to stay at his side, raising their family.

For good or ill, this was her world now. She lifted her head and took in the spectacular view down the valley to the capital city, ringed by snowy mountains. Her gaze moved around the room to centuries-old carved bookcases filled with a mix of leather-covered books and modern office binders. The decorative plasterwork ceiling and huge antique rug that contrasted with and yet complemented the series of modern photographic studies on one wall.

Lucien had stepped into the Kingship, making his own changes along the way.

Start as you mean to go on.

Aurélie shoved the chair back from his desk, ignoring the laptop, and turned to the door. She had a lot to do before this afternoon's tutorials.

'She's where?' Lucien couldn't believe his ears.

'In the centre of the old town. She walked through the pedestrian zone with a pack of photographers on her heels. Now she's in a bookshop. I've organised some security to be there when she comes out, to keep the press back. But their numbers are growing.'

'A bookshop?' Lucien scowled. 'What was so

urgent she had to go out today of all days to buy a book?'

His secretary cleared his throat and offered his phone. 'From what I saw there was no urgency. She took her time.'

Lucien stared at the small screen, the short film clip of Aurélie strolling through the city's most exclusive shopping zone. She looked pale and the high set of her shoulders gave away her tension, but her pace was slow and she took her time window shopping.

His heart rose to his throat and he had to swallow jerkily to find his voice. 'She's gone there deliberately.' Certainty swelled behind his disbelief.

'Then she's a brave woman.'

Lucien nodded, torn between admiration and anger. She shouldn't be doing this alone.

'Organise a car for me. I'll be down in a couple of minutes.' He stood, picking up his own phone and dialling as he reached for his jacket.

He found her in the children's section, apparently engrossed in the book she held. But her head lifted at his footsteps.

'Lucien! What are you doing here?'

'I could ask you the same.' He kept his voice low. 'I told you to stay at the castle.'

Her fine eyebrows rose. 'Was that an order?'

'Of course not. I was trying to protect you.' He'd run the gauntlet of the press clustered outside. His throat clogged as he thought of her facing them alone.

Her expression softened. 'I appreciate it. But I remembered your advice. To start as I mean to go on.' She closed the book with a snap. 'I was afraid if I hid away from them today it would get harder and harder.'

She swallowed and Lucien saw past her raised chin and determined mouth to the upset woman. Distressed because of him.

'Ah, Aurélie.' He lifted his hand to her cheek, stroking gently. 'I'm sorry. This is my fault.'

'Don't be nice to me.' Her mouth wobbled in an approximation of a smile. 'This is tough enough as it is.'

'But you're doing wonderfully. And you look delicious.' It was true. 'That green suits you and I like what you've done to your hair.' He touched a curly strand that feathered her alabaster neck. Her hair was up but not in a rigidly smooth arrangement. Instead it was gathered in a soft-looking knot with a few wispy curls framing her face. 'Sophisticated and sexy.'

Colour streaked her cheeks and her lips twitched. 'I thought it better than a ponytail for this.'

He nodded. 'You look perfect.'

Her mouth turned down. 'Perfect as a king's lover?'

'Perfect for me. And to meet someone important. I spoke to her about you yesterday and planned to take you to see her later. But, in the circumstances, we'll do it now.' He gestured to the book she held. 'Are you buying that?'

Aurélie nodded, picking up another couple of books resting on a low shelf. 'I thought I'd buy my brothers a book each. It didn't have to be done today but…' She shrugged her shoulders.

The brothers who followed their parents in seeing her as a drudge? Aurélie's generosity surprised him.

'You don't have to explain to me.' He paused and met her grave brown eyes. 'I admire you, Aurélie. More than I can say.'

Perfect for me.

Lucien's words carried her through the purchase of the books and out into the cobblestoned square in a haze of excitement and delight. Did he mean it or were they simply words of reassurance?

Common sense decreed the latter, yet the heat of approval in those stunning amber eyes turned her inside out and almost—almost made her believe in miracles. Like the handsome Prince falling for his pregnant commoner Cinderella.

His praise and support lifted her confidence and made her feel good about herself. That had boosted her determination to face the press today.

They were sweeping across the square, reporters trailing them, before she really paid attention to the press scrum. And it was a scrum, even worse than when she'd arrived. The difference was that now there were dark-suited men ensuring they kept their distance.

And Lucien, his hand at her elbow, his tall body solid and reassuring at her side. She tried not to huddle closer, knowing it wasn't the cool breeze that made her want to lean against him.

'Where are we going? Who are we meeting?'

'The only other remaining member of my family. I'd arranged for us to visit her in a few days' time but when I heard you were here, with a press pack in tow, I brought the meeting forward. Remarkably she was free.'

Aurélie had known he must have been informed about her being in the city. He hadn't just happened along. But as they made their way towards an elegant building on the far side of the square, his staff keeping the press at a respectful distance, she realised what she hadn't before. This was a rescue. Lucien had abandoned his schedule to come and protect her.

There was that word again.

He felt protective. Was it madness to hope he might one day feel more?

Perfect for me. His words teased her.

She'd never been perfect for anyone except her mother. It was dangerous to think in those terms. Lucien was a good man, and caring, but he was only making the best of a difficult situation. They were together because she was pregnant. That was all.

The building had huge plate glass windows. On the ground floor she made out acres of display cabinets crammed with delicious treats and beyond that an elegant high-ceilinged room, exquisitely decorated. The patisserie looked as if it belonged in a more gracious age.

'We're going upstairs.' Lucien nodded towards more huge windows and Aurélie caught sight of tables facing out across the square.

'It's very…imposing.'

'It's one of the city's finest restaurants. An ideal place to see and be seen.'

Be seen? Aurélie was hoping to escape public attention for a bit.

A uniformed staff member opened the door with a bow and they headed up a grand crimson-carpeted staircase.

'It feels as opulent as the palace,' she whispered, trying to repress nerves and burgeoning curiosity.

'It's had royal patronage for three centuries. But don't worry, the food is fantastic and the service friendly.' He stopped, passing his coat to a waiter and helping Aurélie out of hers.

Lucien's gaze skimmed her new dress. 'I *do* approve,' he murmured, then looked up. 'Ah, she's already here.'

He ushered her across the spacious room towards a table at the centre window, set apart from the others. It commanded a view of the whole square and up a broad boulevard to the palace.

His fingers squeezed Aurélie's as they stopped before the table, set with damask linen, cut crystal and heavy silverware. A slim woman in a stylish crimson suit surveyed them with shrewd amber eyes. Her hair was white and her hands knobbly with age but her bearing was upright and her aristocratic features firm.

'Aunt Josephine, I'd like you to meet Aurélie Balland. Aurélie, this is my great-aunt, the Grand Duchess Josephine of Vallort.'

Aurélie's heart skipped. Grand Duchess sounded as daunting as King and this old lady's severe stare wasn't welcoming.

Should you curtsey to a grand duchess?

Aurélie decided to treat her as she would anyone else.

'It's lovely to meet you.' She reached out to shake her hand. For an instant she just *knew* she'd done the wrong thing, when that stare turned piercing. Then an arthritic hand lifted and clasped hers in a surprisingly strong grip.

'How do you do?' The old lady turned to Lucien. 'Sit down, do. You'll give me a crick in my neck, looking up so far.'

Instead of being daunted by her complaint, Lucien grinned and bent to kiss her. 'It's good to see you looking so well.'

'And why wouldn't I? Nothing wrong with me, Lucien. I don't have time to be ill.' She paused, frowning, as the waiter approached and murmured something to Lucien.

Lucien shot Aurélie an apologetic look and her heart sank. 'I'm sorry. This will only take a few minutes but I really do need to deal with it.'

The Grand Duchess shooed him away. 'Come back when you can devote your full attention to us. In the meantime we can have a cosy chat.'

The gimlet stare she gave Aurélie looked anything but cosy, but Aurélie told herself it couldn't be worse than facing the press pack shouting questions. Could it?

'So, you're Lucien's young woman. Like the idea of feathering your nest in a royal palace, eh? I gather it's a far cry from your previous life, waiting tables. I'm not surprised you jumped at the chance to hook Lucien.'

Aurélie jerked back in her seat as if she'd been slapped. She hadn't expected to be welcomed with open arms, but nor had she expected this. Naively, she'd thought the worst she'd have to face today was the clamorous press.

'Actually,' she said, knotting her fingers in her lap and lifting her chin, 'living in a palace, or in this case a castle, isn't my preference. Apart from anything else, I don't like the way people think it gives them the right to judge what goes on inside.'

Not wanting to meet that inimical amber stare that should have been like Lucien's but wasn't, she turned to look outside. There, sure enough, was a huddle of photographers, lenses trained on her. If Lucien had booked this table hoping to show her being welcomed into the royal family that was about to backfire terribly.

'If you're looking for sympathy you won't get any. There's a price to be paid for notoriety.'

Aurélie dragged her gaze back, stifling the urge to get up from the table. Running wouldn't help. Besides, why should the words of one sour old woman hurt her? She'd ignored jibes from her father and stepmother and by now all of Europe thought her some tart.

She sighed. 'So I'm learning. Though, believe it or not, I don't want notoriety. Or riches. Or even a palatial nest.' She clamped her mouth shut, realising it was pointless. The Grand Duchess wasn't disposed to like her.

'But you do want Lucien, don't you?'

Aurélie met those bright eyes and denial died on her tongue. To her chagrin she felt heat flood her cheeks.

'You'll have to try camouflaging that high colour of yours or everyone will know when you're lying.'

Aurélie shook her head. 'I don't lie.'

'You're saying you care for him? Do you love him?' she snapped out, leaning across the table.

'Yes, I do,' Aurélie snapped back.

Her eyes rounded as she realised what she'd admitted. She swivelled her head towards the stairs where Lucien had disappeared but there was no sign of him.

'Ah, now that makes it interesting. Does he know?'

Mutely Aurélie shook her head.

'And yet he wants to marry you.' At Aurélie's stunned look she nodded. 'He told me of his plans. To be honest I couldn't work out why he was so set on marriage. Unless...' Her gaze dropped to Aurélie's waist and Aurélie felt her cheeks burn. Nevertheless she kept her chin up and her mouth closed.

Finally the Grand Duchess spoke. 'You're not as I'd feared, Ms Balland.'

'It would be nice to think that was a good thing. But the way my day's going, that would be too much to expect.'

To her amazement, the old lady gave a sharp crack of laughter that echoed across the room. In her peripheral vision Aurélie registered heads turning.

'It's definitely a good thing. I like you, Ms Balland. I hadn't expected to, but you're everything Lucien said and more.'

Aurélie frowned, wondering what he'd said, and how she'd managed to sway her interrogator.

'I hope you'll forgive my rudeness, my dear. But I have a soft spot for my great-nephew and I'd hate to see him caught by a conniving gold-digger.'

'I'm not—'

'Yes, I can see you're not.'

And to Aurélie's astonishment the Grand Duchess gave her a smile every bit as charming as Lucien's. It transformed her expression from stern to welcoming.

'You were testing me?'

'Someone has to look out for him. He's so busy taking on a burden that was never supposed to be his, I couldn't be sure he was thinking clearly.'

Those amber eyes flickered and for a moment Aurélie thought she read terrible sadness there. Until the old lady seemed to gather herself.

'It's been a terrible time for your family. I'm sorry for your losses.'

The Grand Duchess nodded abruptly. 'Harder for Lucien though. Much harder. But now he has you. If you can stay the course.' Her eyes narrowed and Aurélie felt she was being sized up. 'Being King is no job for a single man. Lucien needs someone who'll support him. Can you do that?'

'I...' She hadn't thought of Lucien needing support. He'd been the one making everything happen. Managing problems. Protecting her. But she remembered his weariness as he'd dealt with the fallout of his broken engagement and it would only get worse. 'The media doesn't like me.'

'The media? Pish! We don't let those hounds rule our lives. This fuss will eventually pass. I'm talking about someone who'll give him stability, companionship, support.'

'I'd like to help him.' If he'd let her. 'But there's

so much I don't know. Rules, politics, etiquette.'
Aurélie gathered her courage. 'For instance, should
I have curtsied to you?'

'Only if you wanted me to think you were toady-
ing. You've got a good firm handshake, excellent
posture and a pleasant smile. More than that, you
can think for yourself and you've got courage.' She
nodded. 'You'll do. And you can come to me for
advice. Good to see you have an eye for colour too.'
She gestured to Aurélie's dress. 'Clever of you to
wear Vallort green. The press will lap it up and lo-
cals will see it as a sign of respect for our country.'

Aurélie didn't have the heart to admit she hadn't
realised the significance of the shade. But looking down the boulevard to the palace she saw the
national flag flying proudly, white and the very
same green.

Was that why Lucien had been so pleased with
the dress? She'd hoped he thought her pretty in it.

But just because they shared spectacular sex
didn't mean he was falling for her. She had to remember that.

'You haven't been trying to scare Aurélie off,
have you?' Lucien murmured as he slid into the seat
beside her, taking her hand in his. Immediately her
stiff body softened. He smiled but a slight frown
wrinkled his forehead.

'Nonsense. The girl has more gumption than to
be frightened by a harmless old lady.'

Aurélie smiled and Lucien snorted with laughter. 'The day you behave like a harmless old lady is the day I start worrying.' Yet he slanted a questioning look at Aurélie.

'We've been having a cosy chat,' she reassured him and caught the Grand Duchess's approving eye.

Remarkably, it seemed she'd discovered an ally. Which was just as well. Aurélie was going to need one.

CHAPTER FIFTEEN

'I can't accept it.' Aurélie dragged her eyes from the jewellery box to Lucien, sitting on the edge of the bed.

His straight shoulders looked wider than ever naked. Her pulse quickened as she saw the tiny marks there. Marks she'd just made with her fingernails as they made love.

'You haven't even seen what's inside.' A smile lifted one corner of his mouth and she cursed the familiar melting sensation deep inside.

'It looks expensive. I don't need expensive gifts.'

For a moment Lucien looked almost disappointed. But she put that down to a trick of the light.

'Occasionally a bit of bling is called for. Tonight is one of those nights. Aunt Josephine's parties are very exclusive and very formal. If you don't wear at least *some* jewellery, you'll draw extra attention to yourself.'

Finally Aurélie nodded, accepting the box he pushed into her hands.

The last couple of weeks had been a trial, with so much public curiosity about her. Luckily she'd had the support of Lucien, his friends and even his indomitable and surprisingly likeable great-aunt.

The spiteful stories had eased a little after Princess Ilsa was photographed leaving a party with a notorious billionaire, apparently for a private rendezvous on his luxury yacht. Stories about her being heartbroken over Lucien couldn't survive in the face of what looked like a blatant affair with a hot lover.

Plus the press who'd tried to dig up dirt on Aurélie had come up empty-handed. People from her home town had been generous with praise. Even her family had for a change been positive. Her stepmother had got quite teary about how much they missed her!

Her family had called to wish her well. The boys had been excited and full of questions about life in a castle but her father and stepmother had been subdued. They would never be close. Aurélie told herself she'd concentrate on the new family she was making with Lucien.

'Aurélie?'

She opened the box. Then froze.

'This is for *me*?' Her voice sounded strangled.

It was dazzling. Two rows of lustrous pearls made a choker style necklace. At the front, surrounded by brilliant diamonds, was a huge aqua gem. Yet when it moved in her shaky hand highlights of deeper green, cobalt and even crimson glowed.

'It looks alive.'

'It's an Australian opal. You like it?'

Aurélie swallowed. Like didn't go anywhere near her feelings. 'It's the most beautiful thing I've ever seen.'

She looked up and found Lucien watching with such intensity her breath stuttered. This wasn't simply a kind gesture, like arranging the piano lessons she so enjoyed.

This was the sort of gift a man gave the woman he loved.

Was it possible?

She licked suddenly dry lips and Lucien's attention dropped to her mouth. Her blood sizzled.

'It will look perfect with that aqua dress you've been saving for tonight.'

He'd chosen it because it matched her *dress*?

She'd hoped he'd think *she* was perfect, not her wardrobe. That he'd see not the image she projected but the woman desperate for his love. He'd described her as perfect once, but then too he'd meant appearances.

Aurélie's stomach hollowed as she stifled disappointment. 'It's an expensive gift just to match my dress.'

Their gazes caught and held. Anticipation rose.

'Appearances are important. I know you're still not comfortable at court but wearing this will help you look the part.'

Hope crumbled and Aurélie berated herself for a fool. How could she have thought…?

She looked down at the gems before he could read her distress. This was window dressing to help her look as if she belonged.

'Besides, in two days you'll be twelve weeks

pregnant and we'll announce our engagement.' He paused as if awaiting a response. 'Look on it as an early engagement gift. You'll need something special to wear for the official photos.'

Lucien was being thoughtful, ensuring she'd look the part tonight and next week when they officially got engaged.

Even so, a great ache started up in Aurélie's chest. Thoughtful was nice. But it was no substitute for love.

She nodded, stroking the fiery opal rather than meeting Lucien's eyes. There was no point pining for the impossible. Lucien *cared*. That had to be enough. And he wanted her physically.

Maybe that was why she felt so needy. Making love always made her feel emotionally close to him, though for him it was just lust.

'You're right. It will look terrific with the beaded dress.'

'Stand up and I'll put it on you.'

Aurélie slid out of bed and turned so he stood behind her. She looked through the open dressing room door to their reflections in a full-length mirror. Her pale body and messy hair contrasted with Lucien's taller, stronger frame, his golden skin. Her heart dipped as he swept her hair aside, settling the necklace around her throat and fastening the catch.

He was right. Even naked, the piece transformed her into someone else.

Like the sort of woman he'd have chosen for

himself if an unexpected pregnancy hadn't forced his hand?

Aurélie swallowed convulsively.

'You're so sexy.' Lucien's voice was a gruff rumble that twisted her insides needily.

For her it wasn't only sex, it was love too. Maybe that was why, despite her turmoil, she found it impossible to resist when he wrapped an arm around her waist and hooked her back against him. His other hand went to her breast. Desire weakened her as she watched him tease her nipple and felt the deft play of his fingers on her flesh. Threads of fire wound through her and she shifted back against his erection.

In the mirror their eyes met, Lucien's glazed with hunger. He looked magnificent. Strongly muscled, handsome and sensual. His heavy-lidded stare was pure invitation.

Need ignited. She wanted *not* to want him. *Not* to love him. But there was no remedy for it.

'I want you, Aurélie.' His arm dropped from her waist and she watched it slide down her still-flat abdomen, into her nest of red curls. She was already wet, muscles clenching around his fingers as he delved then withdrew. Her knees loosened.

This man made her weak. But she wanted to be strong. Strong enough not to care that he didn't love her.

She reached around and grasped him, fingers sliding down his length.

That solid jaw clenched and his neck arched back as he groaned. The sound elicited a thrill of pleasure at her power. It made her feel less helpless, watching the tendons stand proud in his taut throat, feeling the jerky thrust of his body into her hand.

'I need you. Now.' It was a gruff demand. Lucien stepped back, holding her against him as he sat abruptly on the bed.

The hair on his thighs tickled the back of her legs as she sat but her focus was on his jutting arousal behind her.

'Spread your legs.' Aurélie didn't refuse. She wanted this. Large, impatient hands splayed her legs wide so she sat astride him, open to his touch. She gasped as he delved again to her core, teasing till she shivered and her eyelids fluttered.

'Keep your eyes open, Aurélie. Look at us.'

Through the open dressing room door she saw their reflection. She looked utterly wanton, naked and spreading herself to his touch. Her legs were wide across his thighs, his hand teasing her clitoris as she rocked against him. Her inner muscles spasmed at the picture they made, his face looming behind her, taut with primal hunger.

'Lift up, sweetheart, and let me in.'

Aurélie rose then sank slowly, savouring the thick thrust of his erection, piercing deep. She shuddered as he shifted and ripples of arousal spread.

He moved again, urging her up. She rose then fell again, harder this time, and sensation rioted through her. In the mirror she watched his hands cup her breasts as he grazed her neck with his teeth and pinched her nipples. Aurélie jerked forward, needing friction, and his hand was there again, rubbing while he filled her from behind, pushing hard and insistent till everything exploded in a desperate rush to ecstasy.

She heard him shout, felt his teeth on her flesh, his thrusting weight fill her to the limit, and rapture took them both.

An age later he spoke. She was too spent even to open her eyes, just lolled against him, not wanting to move.

'You didn't want to marry for our child's sake, Aurélie, but there are bonuses, don't you agree?'

Her eyes opened then to see herself spread, boneless, across his big frame, his grin one of satiation.

Sex was a bonus, not some spiritual connection. They would marry for their child's sake. Clear and simple.

So much for her pathetic hopes.

Lucien looked across the glittering crowd to his fiancée and fought a frown.

It had been a good night. Josephine's parties were always terrific, with interesting people and engaging conversation. Aurélie had fitted in beautifully and appeared to enjoy herself. They'd drifted apart after she'd insisted he didn't have to stay by her side all night.

Funny how that had struck a jarring note. He *wanted* to be with her. But seeing her conversing with various guests, her smile engaging, he knew she'd been right. He couldn't be by her side all the time, no matter how much he wanted to be. She needed to forge some relationships of her own.

Yet he'd felt unsettled since they'd left the castle. They'd had stupendous sex and Aurélie had been suitably dazzled by his gift. She wore it now with a strappy beaded dress that caressed her curves and glittered when she moved. She looked a million dollars.

Yet something wasn't right. Despite her smiles this evening. Despite the passion. He thought back to the scene in his bedroom and how, even as they'd shared that awesome climax, he'd felt a change in her. A shift away from him.

It was impossible. Two people couldn't get closer than they'd been. He'd *felt* it, damn it! He'd fought for weeks to break down Aurélie's barriers and thought he'd succeeded. Now he wasn't sure.

The strange thing was that, while he'd tried to dismantle those barriers, she'd sneaked under his guard and made him feel things he hadn't thought possible. He knew the acute ache that came from losing loved ones and had guarded his emotions, wary of feeling too much. He'd been spectacularly unsuccessful.

Tuning out the conversation around him, he narrowed his gaze on his fiancée. She looked pale and there were tiny vertical lines on her brow.

Excusing himself, he crossed the room, his hand sliding around her elbow. She was trembling and instantly leaned into his hold.

'Will you excuse us?' Without waiting for an answer, Lucien led her from the room, his arm around her waist.

'What is it?' he asked when they were alone. 'Morning sickness?'

'No, I—' Her breath hissed and her hand went to her abdomen. 'I need the bathroom.'

Quickly he shepherded her there then paced the corridor, staring at but not seeing the artwork on the walls. Instead he saw the downward tug of Aurélie's lips as if she were in pain.

She'd be okay. Of course she would. Perhaps the finger food hadn't agreed with her. Yet he paced again, too restless to settle. His nape prickled and apprehension blocked his gullet.

Finally the bathroom door cracked open. Lucien was there in two strides. His blood chilled as he read Aurélie's milk-white face.

'Please, I need the hospital.' Her mouth twisted. 'The baby…' She put out a hand and he grabbed it, steadying her.

'It'll be all right,' Lucien murmured, telling himself it *must* be, as his brain clicked through the mechanics of getting her to hospital as soon as possible. Fear stirred but he thrust it down. He didn't have that luxury when Aurélie needed him. 'Everything will be fine, you'll see.'

He pushed the door open, lifted her into his arms and turned towards the entrance.

Soft curls nudged his neck and chin as she shook her head. 'It won't,' came the stifled sob. 'I'm bleeding and there are cramps.' Her voice rose on a gasp of pain and terror.

Lucien's stride faltered and his blood turned icy, then he quickened his step.

'Lucien?' It was Josephine, stepping out from the drawing room, her eyebrows raised.

'Aurélie's unwell,' he said without stopping. 'Ring the hospital. Tell them we're coming. It may be a miscarriage.' His voice cracked.

'An ambulance,' Aurélie whispered, her breath warm and strangely reassuring against his throat. Nothing bad was going to happen to her. He wouldn't let it.

'It's not far and my car's outside. We'll be there in the time it'd take them to reach us.'

And they were. Fortunately his aunt lived on the side of the city closest to the hospital. As he pulled to a stop at the entrance, emergency staff appeared and within moments Aurélie was being taken inside.

After that events became a blur. Later, all Lucien could remember was the stark fear on Aurélie's face and the need to appear calm, for her sake. Inside he was a wreck. He couldn't believe this was

happening. They might lose the baby. Was Aurélie herself safe?

Guilt scorched him. Had this happened because
they'd had sex tonight? He hadn't been gentle. He'd
been desperate to possess her. Or maybe it was the
stress she was under, plus him taking her to the
party. Maybe if she'd rested at home instead... Regrets lay heavy on his conscience.

He spoke to staff who were so composed he
wanted to rage at them for not taking this emergency seriously. For it *was* an emergency. Bright
blood stained Aurélie's dress and her pain was terrible to watch. Lucien did what he could, held her
hand, reassured, answered the staff's questions
when she wasn't up to it.

There were murmured consultations, tests, more
tests, more questions.

Finally, in the early hours, they were alone. Senior staff had been and gone. They'd been grave
and couldn't give firm assurances. What they did
say, what Lucien clung to, was that Aurélie hadn't
miscarried.

Yet.

He swallowed, pain searing his dry throat, and
blinked to clear his vision.

'You should go home and get some rest.' Aurélie
sounded wrung out.

'I'll stay with you.' Somehow he conjured a
smile, pretending that her strained face, as white
as her hospital gown, didn't terrify him.

'You need rest too. Who knows what tomorrow will bring?' Her mouth trembled and she swallowed. She looked so pitiful his heart wrung. 'If you go, I'll try to sleep too.'

'Good idea. I'll settle in the corner so I don't disturb you.'

But she shook her head. 'Please, Lucien. I need to be alone for a little while.' Something must have showed on his face because she hurried on. 'You've been marvellous. But I need…space. They'll call you if there's any change.'

She looked so horribly vulnerable. How could he deny her? Finally he nodded.

He leaned over and brushed his mouth against hers, taking heart from the way her lips clung.

'Call me any time. I'll have my phone on.'

Reluctantly he straightened. He had no intention of leaving the hospital but he'd respect her desire for space. Though it felt totally wrong leaving her.

As he reached the door she spoke. 'If the worst happens. If I lose the baby…' He swung around to see her lips form a crooked line of distress. 'There'll be no need to marry.' Her gaze skittered away. 'I'll go straight home to France.'

Her words tore through him like a grenade through unprotected flesh. Shockwaves ricocheted across his bones. His belly hollowed then filled with bone-freezing ice. How could she even *think*…?

Lucien was halfway back to the bed when her upraised hand stopped him.

'Please, don't argue. Not now.'

Lucien stared down into taut features. Saw the rapid rise of her breasts, the clenched-knuckled grip on her sheet.

Everything urged him to protest, persuade, demand. She couldn't go back to France. He wouldn't allow it.

But she was growing more distressed the longer he stood there. And distress couldn't be good for her or the baby. Lucien breathed deep, nostrils flaring. It shouldn't be possible to detect her floral scent over the antiseptic hospital smell yet it was there. Teasing him with all he stood to lose.

It felt as if someone had plucked his still beating heart halfway out of his ribcage. It thundered high in his throat and his skin felt clammy. His hands clenched but he resisted the urge to reach for her.

'Rest now, Aurélie. We'll talk tomorrow.'

He strode from the room.

Only when he was out of sight did he sag back against the corridor wall. He'd thought he'd plumbed the depths months ago, but this…

Lucien had lost everyone he'd ever loved. Now he faced that prospect again.

CHAPTER SIXTEEN

FROM HER HOSPITAL bed Aurélie stared out over the rooftops to the valley beyond. She could even pick out Lucien's castle in the distance.

She blinked and felt her mouth crumple, helpless tears pooling and blurring her vision. She hated feeling so emotional. Despite the doctor's cautious optimism this morning, it was too early to believe everything would be okay.

Her hand crept across her abdomen.

Was her baby safe?

She thought of Lucien last night. His concern. His determination to look after her.

He was worried about the baby.

Their relationship was predicated on her pregnancy. Last night she'd got ridiculously hopeful, thinking that fabulous opal necklace could be a love token.

Because she'd fallen in love with him at first sight she'd hoped for a miracle.

Lucien had set her straight. He wanted her suitably dressed at glamorous functions and for their engagement photos. He didn't want her looking like a waitress, a pregnant working-class woman, but a royal.

As if even the most gorgeous jewellery could turn her into someone she wasn't.

Her mouth twisted. No jewellery would make her into the sort of woman Lucien could love.

Her hopes had finally died last night when he'd left her. Though she'd asked him to.

If he loved her, he'd have stayed.

If he cared about *her*, he'd have been horrified at her decision to leave if she lost the baby. He'd have told her he wanted her, baby or not.

Yet after an initial objection he'd nodded and left.

What had she expected? A vow of undying affection?

She hadn't been testing him. She'd just stated facts.

Hadn't she?

A convulsive sob escaped. It was clear where she stood. Nothing had altered.

To Lucien her value was solely as mother to his child. As an individual she wasn't worth fighting for.

She rubbed her hand across her face, smearing the tears that leaked down her cheeks.

The door opened and a nurse entered. She pretended not to see the tear tracks, instead greeting Aurélie with a smile and telling her she'd come to help her freshen up. 'The castle sent through a bag for you. You'll be much more comfortable wearing your own things.'

Aurélie looked at the designer suitcase, so different to her battered backpack. Lucien's housekeeper had probably filled it with those lovely silk nightgowns the stylist had organised. What she really wanted was the comfort of the baggy old T-shirt she used to sleep in.

She offered the nurse a wobbly smile. She couldn't afford to mope. She had to be strong and hope for the best. That her baby would be okay. Everything else, like Lucien's feelings for her, was secondary.

By the time she was clean, changed and resting back against the pillows, Aurélie was exhausted. But she roused as the nurse congratulated her.

'Sorry? I don't understand.' It couldn't be for the pregnancy, not while they waited to see if she miscarried.

'On your engagement.'

'Engagement?' Aurélie frowned.

'It's in today's paper.' The woman beamed. 'And so romantic. It's good to think of the King finding happiness after so much loss. We're all so excited for you both.'

Aurélie's brain froze. An engagement, announced in the paper?

There'd been a terrible mistake. Lucien had agreed to wait until next week. Given the danger of a miscarriage, surely he'd wait even longer, because there might *be* no baby. Without a baby, there'd be no engagement, no marriage.

Again Aurélie had to blink back tears.

'Now, now.' The nurse took Aurélie's hand, checking her pulse. 'I know it's scary, being here, but you're doing well this morning. Truly. Rest and try not to worry.'

Aurélie conjured a wobbly smile. 'Thank you.'

When the nurse left she curled up on her side and shut her eyes, though sleep would be impossible. How could she not worry when everything was going wrong? How had the press learned their secret? No one had known—

'Aurélie?'

Her eyes snapped open and there was Lucien. Her heart gave a thump of joy and the cramping pain in her chest eased.

The lower part of his face was shadowed with beard growth, emphasising the masculine angles of chin and jaw. Even the concern etched around his eyes only made him look less like a fantasy hero and more like the man she loved.

Till she remembered his concern was all for the baby she carried, not her.

'You're here early.' Her voice was husky. The sound undid him. He could bear most things, but Aurélie hurting…

Lucien crossed to her bedside and pulled up a chair, yet he didn't reach for her. She looked so fragile.

Seeing the change in her made his chest ache. He wanted to haul her into his arms and reassure himself as much as her. He wanted to make things better for her but some things were beyond his control. He wasn't even sure how to reach her when she wore that shuttered look.

But he had to try. More, he had to *succeed*. He refused to consider the alternative, of her shunning him permanently.

'I stayed the night.' Seeing her stunned look he clarified. 'The chairs in the waiting room are surprisingly comfortable.' Or would be if you weren't well over six feet. 'I had someone bring clothes for us both this morning.' He rubbed his stubbly chin. He'd forgotten to ask for a razor.

Her red-rimmed eyes rounded. 'You could have gone to the palace. Someone would have rung if there was a change.'

Lucien shrugged. 'I wanted to be here.'

Not wanted but *needed*. He couldn't stay away.

The staff had got used to him prowling the corridor through the night, checking on Aurélie through the window in the door and demanding updates whenever staff checked on her.

Fortunately the news this morning was more positive. He clung to that.

'I hear you're doing well today. You and the baby.'

Aurélie's gaze slid away. The connection he'd felt from the moment she'd met his eyes frayed.

'We've got a problem.'

'The baby?' He reached out and took her hand. To his horror she flinched.

What was that? He was used to Aurélie melting

in his embrace, snuggling up to him, not shrinking away. His fingers tightened, *willing* her to accept his touch. Needing it.

She shook her head, her mouth a tight line.

'What is it, Aurélie? Tell me.' A chill enveloped him. 'Is there some complication? Are *you* in danger?' The doctor hadn't mentioned anything, but a nurse had just been in here. Maybe she'd seen something…

'No, nothing like that. I'm okay.'

Solemn brown eyes met his and his racing heartbeat settled a little. He sank back in his seat, still cradling her hand.

'The press know about our engagement. Did you have a press release ready? That must have been it—'

'That's what's bothering you?'

'Of course!' She frowned. 'It's complicated everything. What if the baby…?' Her mouth folded in tight at the corners and she swallowed. 'What if I miscarry?'

'Whatever happens I'll be with you, Aurélie. I won't leave you again.'

Lucien silently castigated himself. He should have stayed with Aurélie, despite her protests. She was fretting about things that didn't matter.

'Don't you see?' She sat up straighter, colour whipping her cheeks. 'It complicates everything. With this news the media will be even more full of gossip.'

Lucien surveyed her taut features. Her distress was a danger, surely, to herself and their baby.

'Don't worry about the media, Aurélie. Your safety, and our child's, are more important than any news story.'

For a moment those brown eyes met his with something like hope. Then her mouth crumpled.

'If I lose the baby there'll be no engagement. If only they hadn't found out—'

'They were going to find out soon anyway.' Lucien drew a deep breath and folded his other hand around hers, cradling it in both of his. 'I can't apologise for releasing the news.'

It had been a calculated, deliberate action.

'*You* did it?' Shock etched her features. 'But why?'

Grimly he acknowledged his timing hadn't been ideal, but he'd had no choice. He hoped she'd understand and forgive. He'd gambled everything on that action.

The knowledge of what he stood to lose twisted his stomach in knots. He'd never been so frightened.

After months devoted to duty, to meeting the demands of his country, acting in the way his family would have expected and putting his own desires last, Lucien had rebelled. He'd acted selfishly. Yet he couldn't regret it.

He was no saint. Self-sacrifice had limits.

'Because I was desperate.' He'd feared admitting

it but now that didn't matter. All he cared about was Aurélie.

She frowned as if he were a puzzle she couldn't fit together. Not surprising when he hadn't explained. Lucien gathered himself, sitting straighter.

'Last night I was scared.' Terrified would be a better description. Even now he was on edge, hyper-alert. 'When you said you'd leave if you lost the baby, I panicked.'

Aurélie's expression gave nothing away except shock. At least she hadn't pushed him away.

Lucien shook his head. 'That makes it sound like I acted without thinking, and yes, I made a snap decision. But I knew exactly what I was doing when I put through the call.'

'I understand you were worried about the baby, but not why you told the press we were engaged.'

'*Are* engaged.' He paused, heart thundering, waiting for a confirmation that didn't come. He forced himself to continue, despite the glacial chill around his heart. 'Yes, I'm worried about the baby. I don't want to lose it and I worry about how you'd cope if we did. But more than that, I don't want to lose *you*.'

Aurélie's fingers twitched in his hand. 'I don't think there's a big risk to my health from a miscarriage.'

'I mean I don't want you to go back to France. I want you to stay here, with me, no matter what happens with the baby.' He paused, knowing she'd think his action arrogant, whereas in fact he'd been desperate. 'I wanted to force your hand.'

'Why would you want that?' Her fingers curled around his so hard he felt the bite of her short nails.

'Because I want to spend my life with you, of course. I love you, Aurélie.'

There, he'd said it. Revealed what had finally become clear to him.

Lucien surveyed her closely, hope fighting fear. She didn't smile back.

The chill spread, icing his bones.

'You can't. It's just sex and sharing this baby.'

A dreadful plummeting sensation stole his breath. Was that all she felt? He'd hoped for more. Surely that way she made love, and it *was* making love, not just slaking physical desire, proved Aurélie felt more.

He gathered his voice. 'That's all you feel for me?'

'I'm talking about *you*. I know you enjoy sex.' She said it briskly as if she'd never felt that phenomenal shared ecstasy, and something gave way inside him. 'The only reason we're together is because I got pregnant. I even had to prove it was yours with a paternity test. You didn't trust my word. Hardly the action of a man in love.'

As she said it, Aurélie knew how unfair that was. Any man in Lucien's situation would want proof.

Clearly he now knew the child was his. He was pretending he loved her to keep her and the baby here.

Aurélie blinked and concentrated on not giving in to futile tears.

'There was no paternity test.'

Their gazes locked. She told herself he was deliberately using her weakness for him, trying to cajole her into believing him. But it wouldn't work.

'Of course there was. The doctor took my blood the first morning I was here.'

Lucien looked back from under lowered brows, his bright eyes somehow dimmed. 'Yes. But when she approached me about a DNA swab I refused. It felt wrong. I didn't need a test because I knew you were telling the truth.'

'You knew…?' Aurélie had to be hearing things. 'How could you know?'

Those straight shoulders rose. 'I have no idea. Just like I don't understand how I trusted you that first night or why you took the risk of inviting me into your home when you knew nothing about me.' He looked down at her hand, dwarfed between his. 'From the first there's been something between us that defied logic. Connection. Trust. A link. Whatever it is, it's real and I trust it.'

Lucien breathed deep, his chest expanding mightily, and Aurélie felt her own lungs swell on an in-caught breath. The hair at her nape rose. So often she'd pondered the link she'd felt to a man she barely knew. Now she knew him better she understood she'd fallen in love but—

'You really don't know for sure if this is your baby?'

'Oh, I know, Aurélie. It's ours. Because you say so. You'd never pass off another man's child as mine.'

He lifted her hands to his mouth and kissed first one then the other and tendrils of need blossomed, despite her determination to hold strong.

'I hope with everything I am that our baby survives and we can all grow together as a family. But even if the worst happens, I want you with me, as my wife. Not because I want a queen but because I love you.'

Her heart fluttered as if it was about to burst out of her ribcage and escape.

His expression. The look in his eyes. The hammering pulse at his throat. The way his hands shook as they held hers. All chipped away at her certainty that this was a ruse.

'We only met three months ago—'

'I know. I'm asking a lot of you and I'll understand if you don't feel the same way about me yet, but give me time, Aurélie. Stay with me and—'

'I don't want time.'

Before her blurring eyes Lucien's proud face paled. His serious expression turned sombre, as if he'd heard grievous news.

She hurried on. 'You really love me?' Even now it didn't seem possible.

He swallowed hard then nodded.

'Oh, Lucien!' She pulled one hand free of his death grip and cupped his hard jaw. Beneath the prickle of stubble she felt a muscle work and the frantic beat of his pulse. 'I've been so miserable because I thought you only wanted our child. I wanted you to want so much more.'

The transformation in his face was like a blinding flash of sunlight.

'Tell me.' It was a rough command and Aurélie adored the sound.

'I love you, Lucien. I think I've loved you since—'

Aurélie never finished. His mouth slammed into hers and for a long time there was nothing but the desperate need for reassurance between them both. The shared shock of realising their love was mutual. The frantic joy that made them cling to each other.

As the minutes passed and the panicked need for reassurance eased, their kisses grew tender. Lucien caressed her face, his touch soft as he brushed hair from her cheeks.

She looked into his eyes and now she saw it. Something she hadn't seen since her mother. A light that eclipsed all else.

A light that warmed her right to the core of her being.

Aurélie had come home. She was wanted, truly

wanted, not for something she could provide but for herself.

She'd found love.

'I've never been so happy,' she murmured between kisses.

'Nor have I.' Lucien's voice was tender yet serious. Eyes the colour of sunshine and promises smiled down into hers. 'This is only the beginning, my darling. Only the beginning.'

EPILOGUE

'AND SO, MY FRIENDS, I give you our beloved King Lucien. May his next ten years on the throne be as peaceful and successful as his first ten.'

Lucien's chest swelled with pride. Not because of Aurélie's kind words about his first decade as King, but because of *her*.

Seeing her on the royal podium in the vast ball-room, poised and lovely as she addressed the crowd in all three of Vallort's official languages, Lucien wanted to sweep her into his arms. To kiss her with all the wild passion nine and a half years of marriage hadn't dimmed.

A vision in brilliant aqua, in a gleaming sleeve-less ball gown, wearing her favourite opal choker necklace and a delicate opal and diamond tiara in her bright hair, she was everything to him.

Almost everything. A small hand twisted in his and he looked down to meet earnest brown eyes beneath copper hair.

'That's you, Papa! King Lucien.' Five-year-old Prince Alex's voice was almost drowned by the swell of sound as the throng repeated Lucien's name in a toast.

'So it is.' Lucien smiled.

'He'll have to go up there to make a speech. You'd better take my hand instead, Alex.' At nine years old, Justin had a royal's upright posture and sense of responsibility. At least at official occasions. The rest of the time he was usually haring around with his friends, getting into mischief. He was also, according to Aurélie, the very image of Lucien.

'Or,' said a third voice, 'we could *all* go and join *Maman*. She might be lonely up there by herself.'

Lucien tried and failed to suppress a smile as he met his daughter's beguiling gaze. Another redhead like her mother, seven-year-old Chloe knew far too much about how to get her own way. But she was good-natured as well as smart, with a cheeky sense of humour. She was hard to resist.

Lucien looked up to see his wife watching him with raised eyebrows.

'An excellent idea, Chloe,' he said, ushering the children forward. 'We'll all go.'

Seconds later, Lucien stood on the podium with his children before him and his sweetheart at his side. He held her closer than royal tradition dictated. But certain traditions had changed in the last decade.

Among the celebrating crowd he saw not one shocked face that he'd bring his brood to the anniversary ball.

To one side of the room, with a glass of champagne in her hand, sat Great-aunt Josephine, regal in crimson, her eyes sparkling.

'After Papa's speech we can dance, can't we, Papa?'

'One dance only,' Aurélie whispered, 'then it's bedtime.'

His wife might be the one with the psychology degree but Lucien had enough experience as a father and a diplomat to know it was time to begin his speech. Before the complaints began.

He spoke briefly but warmly before inviting the crowd to enjoy the rest of the night.

Lucien danced with his daughter and both boys waltzed with their mother. Justin even persuaded Aunt Josephine onto the floor, to the delight of onlookers.

Finally, Lucien held his beloved wife in his arms, whirling her down the length of the gilded ballroom.

'Have you danced with the new English ambassador yet?' she murmured in his ear. 'She has a soft spot for you.'

Lucien bent his head, inhaling Aurélie's fresh flower scent, the same after all these years. 'I will on one condition.'

'What's that, Your Majesty?' Sultry dark eyes met his and heat shot straight to his groin.

He growled under his breath, 'Don't rush to take off that necklace when we go upstairs.'

Aurélie's eyebrows rose in mock surprise. 'But I can't sleep in it, Lucien.'

He hauled her closer and bent to murmur against her lush mouth, 'It's not sleep I have in mind.'

Then, as he whirled her round the end of the ball-

room, her dress flaring out against his legs, Aurélie's laugh pealed out and his heart soared.

They might have fallen for each other in a single
night but what they shared grew better and better.
No man looked forward to the future more.

* * * * *

Caught up in the drama of
Pregnant with His Majesty's Heir?
Why not also take a look at these
other stories by Annie West?

Revelations of a Secret Princess
Contracted to Her Greek Enemy
Claiming His Out-of-Bounds Bride
The King's Bride by Arrangement
The Sheikh's Marriage Proclamation

All available now!